About the Author

My initials 'GG' stand for Grumpy Grandad which is the name I was called by my grandchildren when they were of the best age to hear my stories and beg for pocket money, which they did. But I was telling my first Josser story long before they came along, when I was very young teacher trying to control a class in the East End without the aid of a big stick.

Storytelling was used as a kind of bribe. If they were good to me during their lessons, I would end the day with a story, making sure to be at the most exciting point when the bell rang. The class would go home wondering what might happen next, and saying I did that on purpose.

Josser's Door

GG

Josser's Door

Olympia Publishers
London

www.olympiapublishers.com
OLYMPIA PAPERBACK EDITION

A CIP catalogue record for this title is
available from the British Library.

ISBN: 978-1-83934-099-4

First Published in 2021

Olympia Publishers
Tallis House
2 Tallis Street
London
EC4Y 0AB

Printed in Great Britain

For Kai

Chapter 1
The Disappearing Sausage

Josser had been digging all day. He had almost finished digging a tunnel under the roots of a big oak tree, and was looking forward to turning his tunnel into a snug home for his brother, Mel, and himself. He was also looking forward to his supper; digging made him hungry.

He knew exactly what he was going to have for supper. A sausage, which he would cook himself. His mouth was already watering at the thought of biting into a crisp, golden brown sausage. He could see it, in his mind, sizzling in his frying pan. He could taste it as, in his mind, he bit into it. Josser loved sausages, and felt it was a great pity he had only two left, and must reserve one for a very special occasion.

So he climbed out of the tunnel and put down his spade. He washed his hands in his water bucket, and raked his cooking fire so the embers glowed, before heaping them around the stone which served as his hob. He smeared some lard in his frying pan, and watched it melt after he had placed the pan on the hot hob. Only when the lard was all melted and he could hear it sizzle did he drop in the sausage.

"Tomato sauce," he said, remembering he might have just a smidgeon left. He went back into to his tent, and rummaged through all his untidy belongings until he found the almost empty bottle under his second-best hat.

"Just enough for two more sausages," he told himself, knowing he must make sure the very last smidgeon of tomato sauce was reserved for that very special occasion. Then he went back to his cooking fire to turn the sausage over so it would be crisp and golden brown everywhere.

But, when he looked in the pan it was empty. There was no sausage. The sausage had gone.

"Where's me sossidge?" Josser shouted. "Somebody's swiped me sossidge!"

He spoke like that because when he was excited he forgot both his manners and his grammar; losing his supper had made him very excited. He thought the sausage might have fallen out of the pan by itself because there was no one in sight, so he raked in the fire, but the sausage wasn't there. In vain, he poked around in the grass, and he even looked to see if the sausage had become stuck to the underside of the pan, but it had not. Then he thought it might have tried to escape and was hiding under the bed in his tent. It wasn't.

Josser gave up. He stood outside his tent, and was still scowling when Mel, his brother, came back from fishing.

"Hello!" said Mel. "You do look miserable!"

"Me sossidge has disappeared."

"Sausages do not disappear," Mel said, "Unless they are eaten."

"Mine did. One minute it was happily frying in the pan. The next minute, it wasn't."

"H'm," said Mel, "Frying, you said. Do you know I think I can almost smell fried sausage." Then he sniffed, and his nose twitched, and he murmured, "Yes. I do smell fried sausage."

He put a finger to his lips and silently mouthed these words, "Shush. Listen and do as I say."

He spoke loudly and clearly again.

"Well, brother, you do have another sausage. Put that in the pan, and while it is cooking, we will admire your tunnel."

Josser did what he was told. Before he could argue, because he always liked to argue, Mel had grabbed him by the arm and dragged him away, not to go into the tunnel, but to stand behind the tree and peep.

"Watch," he whispered, and then a little later, he added, "Look up!"

So Josser did as he was told and saw a dangling hook. It was on the end of a line coming down out the branches of the tree, and while Josser watched, the hook moved down, down, and down. Towards his very last sausage. He wanted to rush out and stop it, but Mel held him back.

"Not yet. Not yet," he whispered.

The hook was already swinging backwards and forwards over the pan, sometimes clinking against its side, and sometimes touching the sausage, making it roll, as if it were trying to escape. Then the hook caught, its barb digging into the sausage's crisp, golden-brown skin.

"Oh no!" wailed Josser as his sausage rose slowly from the pan.

"Wait," Mel hissed. Before the sausage could disappear up in the branches, Mel had rushed out and grabbed the line.

He tugged and the branches swayed. He tugged again, this time much harder. There was a crack as a branch snapped, a yell of "Help!", and a body tumbled out of the tree.

It landed with a thump, close to the cooking fire. Then it sat up, and said, "It wasn't me. I'm innocent! It were someone else, mister. And now he's runned away."

"He ran away," Mel insisted, because he believed everyone should speak correctly.

"And," he went on, "I think I know you from somewhere.

Who are you?"

The body which had fallen out of the tree had become a scruffy little urchin in patched and ragged clothes. He was very thin. Shaken, and beginning to snivel, he still managed to answer.

"Cherry, mister. Cherry Bobble, and I never did nothing."

"Ah. Yes. Cherry Bobble, otherwise known as 'Cheeky'," Mel said.

"That's not fair," Cherry protested. "I ain't cheeked no one."

"That's your second double negative," Mel pointed out sternly, "So you must have been rude to someone, if not everyone."

Josser had been trying to scrape the ash off his last surviving sausage which had landed in the cooking fire; this lecture about speaking correctly made him explode.

"Blow your double whatsits," he shouted. "He's ruined me last sossidge. I'll never eat this. And I was saving it for a very special occasion."

"You won't eat it?" Mel asked.

"How can I? It's smothered in ash."

"Give it to the lad."

"What!"

"Well, look at him. Starving just like his sisters. He's just skin and bone."

This suggestion was just too much for Josser.

"Skin and bone!" he shouted. "Skin and bone! When I've finished with him he'll be no more than bone."

He tried to rush at Cherry, but Mel restrained him.

"Think of his hungry sisters," Mel pleaded.

"Yeah," Cherry agreed, having backed away to a safe distance. "All four of them, starving at home."

"Two," Mel corrected sternly.

"Oh," Cherry said. "Well, I'm no good at counting. Never went to school."

"You played truant! Naughty. Very naughty." Mel shook his head.

This exchange proved the last straw for Josser. He hurled the sausage at Cherry.

"Take it. Go away. Don't ever come back. I don't want to see you again. Never."

While the boy scuttled away, Josser sat down with his head in his hands.

"Bang goes me supper," he said mournfully.

"Well, actually," his brother began as he opened his fishing bag, "I did catch something."

Determined to think the worst, Josser did not look up, but muttered, "Let me guess. A tiddler? A teeny tadpole?"

"A trout," Mel told him, "and big enough to feed two."

Suddenly Josser cheered up. His empty tummy rumbled.

"Baked with wild mushrooms," he said hopefully.

"And herbs," Mel promised.

So a little later, when the well-cooked trout had been eaten, and Josser was feeling much happier, they sat and talked.

"You said you were keeping your last sausage for a special occasion. What is it?" Mel asked.

"You shouldn't remind me of me sossidges," Josser said.

"Sorry, but I would like to know," Mel apologised.

"When I finish making our house I am going to have a door with a brass door knocker and a letter box."

"That will give Boff something to think about. I don't believe he has ever made a door with a letter box," Mel remarked.

"Boff will not be making this door. I will," Josser declared.

"Excellent idea!" Mel said, knowing that anything his

brother made would be a total disaster. "So that is going to be your special occasion? Having a letter box?"

"No," Josser replied. "Finishing."

They were silent.

"Finishing," Josser repeated. "Finished looking for somewhere to live. Finished sleeping in a leaky tent. Finished trudging day after day. When did we last sleep under a roof?"

"When we were with the Navs," Mel recalled.

"And what was that like?" Josser asked. "Warm? No. It was freezing. Cosy? We had to lie on hard stone slabs. Dry? Water was dripping off a slimy roof!"

"We were by an underground canal," Mel reminded him.

"Never again," Josser said firmly. "I'm through with wandering and being miserable."

"If I remember rightly, you didn't do much to cheer up others."

"I tried," Josser protested. "I told jokes."

"Nurse Twiggs didn't think your jokes were funny. Especially when little Pipkin cried all night."

"There was nothing wrong with that joke!"

"Pipkin didn't think it was a joke. Telling a little boy the canal was infested with crocodiles who would leap out and bite off his feet. Really."

They were silent again, before Josser sighed and said, "I'm going to miss that sausage."

"Perhaps you can persuade Auntie Bessiburger to make you some more."

"I haven't paid her for those two. Which I haven't eaten."

Josser sounded very gloomy.

"Now I will have to dig her garden again, when I should be working on our house."

"Life is very hard," Mel said, and then he started to laugh.

"So now you think it is funny?" Josser snapped.

"No. No! I've just remembered where I last saw that boy. Oh dear, it is so funny."

For a few moments, because he was laughing so much, Mel could not go on. Finally he stopped laughing and said, "I remember now. He came down to the stream and asked me very politely, "Mister, will you teach me to fish?" So I did. I showed him how to tie a hook to a line." When Mel started to laugh again, Josser glowered. "I don't think that's at all funny," he said.

Chapter 2
Seen by a Biggie

Cherry and his two sisters, Lib and Lus, were tucked up in bed. They had promised to go to sleep as all good children should. Mrs. Bobble, their mother, was looking forward to a quiet hour of relaxation in her armchair, with her aching feet soaking in a bowl of warm, soapy water. But just as she was about to sit back with her eyes closed, and think about absolutely nothing...

"Wah. Wah. I want me Ma! Wah. Wah. I do want me Ma!"

"Go sleep!" Mrs Bobble shouted, but the wailing continued. She shouted again.

"Cherry! Are you annoying your sisters? Stop it. Let them go to sleep. Let me get some rest."

"Ma! It ain't me. I ain't done nothing. It's Lib, and she's crying buckets."

The wailing got louder. Mrs. Bobble pretended not hear.

"Ma! MA!" Cherry sounded desperate.

"What's wrong now?"

"It's Lib, Ma. She banging her head into the pillow."

Mrs. Bobble could hear the thump, thump, and thump.

"Ma!" It was her son again.

"What!!!"

"If Lib keeps on, she's going to bust the bed!"

Mrs. Bobble sighed. She lifted her tired feet out of the soothing water and stood up.

"If this is all about nothing, you'll get what for, all of you."

Then, with her feet still dripping wet, she marched towards

the stairs.

"It ain't me, Ma," little Lus squeaked. "Don't take it out on me."

When Mrs. Bobble reached the bedroom, leaving a trail of damp footmarks all the way up the stairs, her daughters, clutching each other tightly, were wailing and rocking as in a duet. Their brother, his arms clasped round his knees, was hunched on his bed.

"Stop this noise. Now!" Mrs. Bobble shouted, and, forgetting she was barefoot, stamped very hard on the floor.

"Yee-ow!" she yelled. "Now, see what you've made me do. I've broken my foot, and you won't get any breakfast." Then they were all wailing, except for Cherry who was wishing he was somewhere else. Even when they had all stopped crying, Lib refused to say why she had started. Mrs. Bobble finally lost her temper.

"If you don't tell me now, I'll sell you to the rag and bone man," she said. Lus gasped, and even Cherry looked shocked. Lib looked as though she was going to cry again. Instead, she mumbled something in a whisper so faint no one could hear.

"Speak up!" her mother ordered. Lib mumbled again.

"I still can't hear!"

Lib's eyes filled with tears. Her lips trembled but no words came.

"She's telling you she's been seen, Ma." Cherry said the terrible words for her.

His little sisters screamed like banshees, rushed at him and began pummelling him with their clenched little fists. Mrs. Bobble had to pull them apart, and give them all a good shaking before peace was restored. Then she made them all go down stairs and face the wall while she recovered her shattered nerves with a pot of very strong tea.

"What did you mean?" she asked her son.

"She's been seen by a biggie, Ma."

"Snitch," said Lus.

"Sneak," said Lib. "You promised not to tell. I hate you!"

"Is this true? Where did this happen?"

The girls remained silent, leaving their big brother to answer the next question, but not without protests.

"On the Crooked Path, Ma."

"Where you're not supposed to go."

"I wasn't crossing it, Ma. I was hardly on it. Well, just touching a teeny bit," Lib admitted.

"Why?" Mrs Bobble sounded so angry the children dared not speak.

"Why?" she shouted, and banged the table so hard everybody jumped, including the teapot.

"She were playing hops," Cherry said finally.

"Hops," his mother repeated. "You play hops every day, outside our own door. Why go all the way to the Crooked Path?"

"Cos it's flat, Ma," Lib said.

"Flat," Mrs Bobble said. "Flat. I've a good mind to make you flat. All of you."

She sighed. "Oh dear. Now look what you've done. You've wearied me out. Well, that's it. I can't deal with you any more. It's off to Gaffer with the lot of you. Tomorrow afternoon, and if he gives you a whopping what for, I won't shed a single tear. Off to bed now, and I don't want to hear another sound."

This time the children obeyed, leaving their mother to close her eyes and doze in her very comfortable chair, but not before she had brewed another pot of tea.

But, in the morning, when Mrs Bobble went upstairs to wake

her three children, Cherry was not there. Her little girls, speaking as one, and in wide-eyed innocence, said their brother was gone when they woke. They had no idea where, and they didn't love him any more.

"It doesn't matter," Mrs. Bobble told her two little girls. "You are still going to face Gaffer this afternoon, so make sure you wash behind your ears."

"Oh, Ma!" they protested, still speaking as one.

Josser emerged from his tent, yawned and stretched, watched the fleecy clouds flying across a bright blue sky, and knew it was going to be a fine, dry day ideal for digging.

"Today, I will finish my house," he told himself. Then he saw that boy, exactly where he had last seen that boy yesterday, only instead of going away that boy was walking towards him.

"Stop!" Josser shouted. Cherry obeyed.

"Turn around and go away."

Cherry shook his head. "Can't," he said.

"Are your feet stuck to the ground?" Josser roared. "Have you come to steal another sossidge, which I haven't got?"

"I've come for help," Cherry said, and he looked very anxious.

"You want my help, you bring back my sossidge. Be off before I boot you."

And this time Cherry obeyed, slinking off just before Mel appeared.

"What was all that noise about?" Mel asked.

Before Josser could explain, Cherry was back in sight looking very unhappy.

"If you won't do it," he shouted, "I'll have to do it myself, and if you never see me again, you'll be sorry."

Then he marched off, leaving both Josser and Mel utterly astounded.

"What's got into the lad?" Mel wondered.

"No idea," Josser said briskly, "and he's got one thing wrong. I'll be happy never seeing him again."

"You're very hard on him," Mel said.

"No harder than he was on my sossidge. Now are you going to give a hand with our house? I'd like to get on with it today."

"Ah. Well, I would like to, but the trout are biting and we'll both need something for supper tonight."

So Josser was left to get on with his digging, which he did. By midday, when he stopped to scrunch an oatcake and drink a mug of water flavoured with a drop of bramble wine, he was able to tell himself the hard digging was done. His tunnel under the roots of the oak tree had finally become an unfurnished home with a kitchen, a living room, a store room, and two bedrooms, each of which would have its very own window. That boy had been completely forgotten.

But not by everyone. Just when Josser was thinking of having an afternoon snooze, Gaffer was hearing all about Lib being seen by a biggie.

"Cherry was there as well. Wasn't he?" Mrs Bobble said, as she prodded her daughter. Lib nodded.

"Oh dear!" Gaffer said. "Would you like a jelly baby?"

Mrs. Gaffer plonked the jar of jelly babies on the table, and the little girls stared at it.

"Nearly empty," Mrs. Gaffer warned. "Don't know if we'll get any more."

"Our foragers will provide," her husband said, and Mrs. Gaffer sniffed because she did not much like Ferriter who led the foragers.

"Now," Gaffer said to the two little girls, "jelly babies are for little girls who tell the truth."

"Can I have that purple one? I like purple," Lus asked.

"It's not for you. You didn't see the biggie," her mother said.

"I did," Lib said. "I like orange."

"But did the biggie see you?" Gaffer asked. Lib nodded.

"You have to say it," he insisted, his hand on the lid of the jelly jar. Lib took a deep breath before speaking in a rush.

"She said 'I see you.'"

"Have a jelly baby. Both of you," Gaffer said.

When they were both chewing, Lus asked, "Can we go out to play?"

"Of course. Off you go while I talk to your mother."

Mrs Gaffer brought in a pot of tea.

"Where is Cherry?" her husband asked.

"Off somewhere," Mrs. Bobble said. "Dunno. Gets more like his dad every day."

"Pipkin's outside," Mrs Gaffer said, "Maybe he knows."

"This sounds like a job for Josser," Gaffer said. "Pipkin can take him a message and look for your son at the same time."

Mel prodded his brother who was snoring.

"What? What! Oh, it's you," Josser said.

"Thought you were digging," Mel said.

"Finished. Been thinking."

"With your mouth open and snorting?"

"Must have dozed off. What's for supper?"

"Nothing." Josser heard a noise and looked up. He saw Pipkin.

"It's that boy again. Maybe we can eat him."

"I'm not that boy," Pipkin protested. "I am Pipkin, not

21

Cherry. But if you have seen him I would like to know where. And Gaffer wants to see you now. And it's very urgent."

"Go away," Josser told him. "Why do all boys look alike?" Then he sighed. "And I was having a really good think about my door."

He got to his feet and shook himself.

"Leave your door to Boff," Mel advised.

"Certainly not," Josser snapped.

The first thing Mrs Gaffer did when Josser and Mel arrived was to put the jelly jar away on a high shelf. Then Lib had to tell her story all over again.

"Oops!" Josser said when she had finished.

"Oops?" Gaffer repeated.

"Cherry came asking for help. Josser sent him away. They are not friends," Mel explained.

"I have heard about the sausage," Gaffer said.

"Two sossidges," Josser protested, "and now you're going to ask me to find the little rascal."

"And sort out the biggie," Gaffer said very quietly.

"What!" Josser was shocked. "We don't sort out biggies. We keep out of their way. If we see them coming we hide."

"This biggie is only a girl," Gaffer pointed out. "And just think what could happen if she tells all her friends."

"We'd become a tourist attraction," Mel added, "And then we'd have to move out."

"I'm thinking of me!" Josser protested. "Squashed flat. Biggies have big feet. Even the girl biggies."

"She didn't squash Lib," Mrs. Bobble said.

"Why didn't I think of that," Gaffer said. "We should ask Lib."

So the little sisters had to be called in, and that meant the jelly jar had to be lifted down. "But only for the children," Mrs Gaffer insisted.

"She was big," Lib said, between chews.

"They're all big," Josser muttered.

"What else did she do? Besides speak to you."

"She pointed straight at me."

"What did you do?"

Lib shrugged.

"I didn't do nothing," she protested,

"Which means you did something," Mel said. Even though he spoke very gently, his words were enough to start Lib crying. And when Lib cried Lus had to cry as well. The jelly jar had to be opened again before quiet was restored, but even then the little girls could tell them nothing. Everyone feared Cherry had gone looking for the biggie.

"You'll have to do something. Find this girl biggie and talk to her," Gaffer suggested to Josser.

"Definitely," Mel agreed, which did not please his brother.

"Well, I do think you should have gone along with Cherry," Gaffer said. "And I now think you should both find out what has happened to him." That displeased both brothers.

"Go back to where they met, somewhere along the Crooked Path," he added.

"By that big brick hut," Lus piped up and they all stared at her.

"Well, that's where the path is smooth," Lus said, red in the face.

"Sounds to me like all your children were involved," Mrs. Gaffer told Mrs. Bobble.

"Which is why I brought them along," Mrs. Bobble said. "So they could have a good whopping." That caused such a wailing

23

all the men put their hands over their ears. How loud that noise might have become no one will ever know. Just as the little girls were getting into their vocal stride and even making the jelly jar rattle, Pipkin appeared. Alone.

"You didn't find him." Gaffer said.

"Sorry, Mr. Gaffer," Pipkin replied, "But I did find this." He held up a carefully folded sheet of paper on which some letters were written very neatly. The words read 'To Whom It May Concern. URGENT.' The last word was written in red.

Gaffer put on his spectacles to try and read these words, making Mrs. Gaffer sniff because she knew her husband didn't really need spectacles at all. His gold-rimmed pair, which had been picked off a tip by the foragers, were only worn for show.

"You read the rest," Gaffer told Mel, and handed on the opened note because the spectacles were hurting his eyes.

"I found that under a stone," Pipkin said.

"Where?" Josser asked.

"Right in the middle of the path. The smooth bit." Mel cleared his throat and read out loud.

"I have your boy. He is so dirty I have put him in a jar of soapy water. If you want him back you must agree to my terms. Or else. Meet you at this place tomorrow afternoon. PALS."

"It's a ransom note," Gaffer said in disbelief.

"Cherry's been kidnapped," Mel explained.

"He's never that dirty!" Mrs Bobble was very indignant.

"Our brother's been put in a jar. Like a jelly baby," Lib told Lus, who looked horrified.

"What is she going to do with him?" Lus asked.

"Probably eat him," Josser told them, "But don't worry. She won't do that straight away. Probably fatten him up for Kissmas. Eat him with a couple of sossidges."

Whereupon the two little girls screamed, and with their little fists clenched, rushed to pummel Josser.

24

Chapter 03
PALS

Josser and Mel were sitting on a branch. They were high enough up to see all the way down the Crooked Path to the bridge across the stream. That was the way the biggie must come because no biggies lived on this side of the stream. There were no biggies even in the squat brick building on the other side of the path. Josser said it was factory because all the factories he knew were made of bricks. Mel said it could not be a factory because it was too small, and besides factories only worked if there were biggies inside.

"It's an electric sub-station," he declared, only he pronounced 'electric' as 'lectric'. "Sometimes biggies will come and look at it."

"Don't like 'lectric," Josser said. "It can frazzle you all up."

"Not any more," Mel said. "Biggies can buy it in little chunks called batteries or rechargeables which they put in those boxes they stick on their ears."

"How is it you know all these things and I don't?" Josser asked.

"Because I can read. Look at that sign on that gate. It reads 'Strictly private. No admittance unless authorised. Danger. High Voltage.'"

"Wish you knew as much about fishing," Josser grumbled. "If you were as clever at fishing we'd have something for supper."

"Can't catch the fish that doesn't come," his brother said.

"And that's enough chat. We should be thinking about dealing with the biggie."

So they thought about the biggie.

"Maybe she's a collector," Josser suggested. "Dad Bobble disappeared when we arrived here. Maybe she nabbed him and has now got two Bobbles. We should tie all the other Bobbles in a bundle and give her the lot. Then she will go away and leave us in peace."

"If that is a joke, it is one of your worst," Mel said.

"Did I say I was joking?"

Before Mel could answer they saw someone climbing over the gate at the other end of the bridge.

"Here she is. You have to do the talking," he said.

Josser looked at the biggie. She was striding towards them purposefully, her arms swinging, hair neatly brushed and in plaits. She wore very smart jeans and laced up boots. Her yellow T-shirt bore the letters PALS, and she was looking very serious.

"She looks bossy," he said.

"Never mind how she looks. Just remember what Gaffer asked us to do," Mel said. Gaffer, who was a great believer in keeping things simple, had kept his instructions brief.

'Just find out what the biggie wants. Tell her nothing about us. Just arrange another meeting and then come back so we can have a confab.' That was the dwarf's way of saying 'confabulation', a meeting which usually resulted in talking for hours and getting absolutely nowhere. As Josser scrambled down the tree, Mel wondered if his brother would follow Gaffer's instructions to the letter. In Mel's view, everything would depend on his brother's mood, and he had only two. He was either grumpy or very grumpy. After the meeting at Gaffer's house and all that wailing, Mel knew which mood his brother was in. He

26

was very grumpy. So as Josser went to meet the kidnapper, his brother feared the worst, even though he knew nothing at all about the biggie Josser was about to face. But then, who could?

PALS' full name was Penelope Arabella Leamington Spa, and she hated it. Once she had asked her mother why they had to put up with such a long name.

"Ask your father, dear," her mother said in the wearied voice of someone who had given up understanding men many years before. So, Penny, as she liked to be called, had asked.

"Because I changed it," Papa had replied.

"Why?"

"Because no one could pronounce our real name which was Chol-monde-ly. People kept calling us Chumley. Couldn't put up with that so I chose a name everyone knew."

He could have chosen Smith, Penny had thought as she had walked away. From then on, she followed her mother's example and treated Papa as no more than the great provider who had paid for a time-share chalet in the Alps, a small yacht on the Adriatic where they all went to be sea sick, and her very expensive education at a nearby boarding school. Now Papa spent most of his time attending committees or looking for his lost golf balls on the nearest course.

Mel, who knew absolutely nothing of Pals' past or how she thought, watched her stride up to the line he had chalked across the Crooked Path. She stopped exactly on the line, and she looked very determined. Even before Josser had stepped out of the bushes to be seen, Mel had a very bad feeling.

"This is going to go very, very wrong," he whispered to himself.

"I see you," Penny said.

Josser strode up to his side of the line, looked up at her, and said "Likewise."

Penny looked down on him, sniffed, and said in a cold and very clear voice, "You must be that disgusting little boy's father. You're almost as scruffy as him, and you smell!"

"Oh dear!" Mel said to himself, knowing what would happen next, for his brother was going very red in the face.

"His dad! His dad! No, thank you. For all I care, you can fry that little scamp and put him in a sandwich. And I do not smell!"

As he spoke those last few words, Josser clenched his fists and shook them at the biggie. She was unmoved.

"Oh," she said calmly, "It sounds to me as if you do not want him back. In that case I will keep him to show to all my friends. Then we will all come up here and hunt for the rest of you."

Then she turned and marched away.

"Oh no," Mel wailed. He scrambled down the tree shouting, "No! Please! Stop. Come back. He doesn't mean it."

"Yes, I do." Josser shouted. He was still standing at the line, with his arms folded. Mel rushed by him and caught up with the biggie just as she reached the bridge. As she kept on walking, he dashed by her, and scrambled up the gate to turn and look her straight in the face.

"Please don't tell anyone about us," he begged, between deep gasps for breath. He wiped his face and blew his nose.

"Oh dear. This has all gone wrong. Gaffer will be furious."

Then realising what he had done, he put a hand over his mouth before saying "Oops!"

Penny looked at him. Mel tried a smile, but it didn't work for her face was still unfriendly.

"Are you that little creature's father?" she asked.

"What? Who? Oh. Cherry. Oops! I've done it again. Haven't I?" This time his smile was very nervous.

"Done what?" Penny demanded.

"Told you things. Gaffer said we were to tell you nothing."

"So the boy is called Cherry and this Gaffer is his father?"

"No. He is Cherry Bobble and his father went missing during the big march. Perhaps the Black Hats got him. Oh dear, now I'm giving all our secrets away. No more questions. Please."

By then, Josser still scowling and very grumpy, had caught up with them. He had clambered up the gate to sit by Mel. Penny stared at them thoughtfully.

"I do believe you are brothers," she said.

"What we are is none of your business," Josser shouted back.

"Oh no!" Mel begged. "I'm sorry, but my brother is not in a good mood. In fact, he is never in a good mood. In fact he only has one mood. Grumpy. Sometimes he's just grumpy but he can have days when he's very—"

"Stop talking," Penny told him. "Both of you listen very carefully. I mean what I say. If you don't agree with my terms I will bring all my friends here and we will skateboard all over this wood, which is not yours in the first place." Faced with this terrible threat even Josser shut up. He and Mel stared solemnly at the biggie.

"Good. Now you are both listening, we can reach an understanding. I will return that boy, cleaned up, in the morning. Half past eight in the morning. On the dot. I will bring him right here, and then you will have two weeks to agree to my terms. We will meet again at the same time, on precisely this very spot. Is that clear?"

The brothers nodded, and then Mel very nervously said, "But we haven't heard your terms yet."

"Of course you haven't because I haven't stated them. They are simple. I come and go anywhere in this wood when I want to.

You don't hide or run away. You will be my secret friends and I won't tell anyone. Now, you can get out of my way because its time I went home for tea."

They meekly climbed down off the gate and stood to one side. They watched in silence as Penny marched away.

"We've been bossed about," Josser said, "and by a girl. Just imagine what she will be like when she grows up. Frightening."

"I'm too busy worrying about what Gaffer is going to say," Mel admitted. "We weren't supposed to tell Pals anything."

"Pals," Josser snorted. "Who would be pals with a biggie like that?"

Gaffer was not amused and Mrs. Gaffer, who felt sorry for Mel, rounded on Josser.

"You could have been polite," she told him.

"She said I was scruffy!" he protested.

"And smelly," Mel muttered, and immediately the brothers were glaring at one another.

Gaffer hurriedly intervened to stop the argument turning into a big row.

"At least she's promised to return Cherry. Will she keep her word, I wonder?"

"Half past eight in the morning," Mel said, "Bang on the dot."

"None of our clocks tell the same time. They're all different," Josser pointed out.

"Then you will be there early," Gaffer told him.

"And this time do try to be polite," Mrs. Gaffer added.

It was still misty when they walked down to the gate. They were both grumpy. Josser, because he could be working on his house, and Mel because he could have been fishing somewhere along the stream. They were also feeling cold because the mist was hiding the sun.

"It's always us," Josser grumbled. "Why is it always us?"

"Well, you did send Cherry away when he came asking for help."

"He didn't say why, did he? How could I help if he didn't say why?"

They were about to get into another argument, just like brothers do, when they were disturbed by a lot of noise coming from behind them.

"We've got company," Mel said.

As they turned to see who was following them, the mist began to lift. The sun was shining down on them, and they felt a little warmer and friendlier.

"It's Mrs Bobble and her two little girls," Mel said.

"They're as bad as Cherry," Josser grumbled because he was still not feeling as friendly as his brother.

The Bobbles were not the only ones coming to welcome back Cherry. A little way behind them was Gaffer, coming to make sure everything was orderly, and even further back was Mrs. Gaffer because she just wanted to know what might happen. She was also telling off Ferriter, who had come along just to see what state Cherry would be in, because she had sent the forager out for jelly babies, and he had returned instead with a packet of chewing gum. Mrs. Gaffer hated chewing gum because after children had chewed the dreadful stuff for hours they were in the habit of sticking it anywhere, which often included the highly polished floor of her tiny little shop.

Ferriter was not happy about being told off. He hated coming back with nothing at all, and had not found even a single jelly baby. He had tried telling Mrs Gaffer that used chewing gum came in handy when you wanted to stick a notice on a wall. That had been a big mistake because he got a long lecture on how it was all very well for men to lie snoring in their armchairs with their feet up while the women did all the washing up, the sweeping, the polishing, made all the meals, and told the children bed-times stories while 'you idle men do absolutely nothing'! So Ferriter was even grumpier than Josser. But he still came along because he had never seen anyone who had been kidnapped by a biggie.

As they approached the bridge, Gaffer said they should go no further. They must wait on their side. According to his clock it had been a minute to eight o'clock when he left home so it must soon be time for the girl biggie to appear. Mrs. Gaffer said she was not surprised their clock showed a minute to eight o'clock, because that had been the time on its face when her husband dropped it months ago. It had not ticked since.

Nothing happened. Gaffer moved to stand by Josser and Mel. He obviously had something very important to tell them.

"When the boy is back with his family and we know what is what, there is going to be a confab. I don't want either of you turning it into a shindig."

"Would we do that?" Josser asked, innocently.

"Couldn't," Mel said, "Not without help."

"You both know what I mean," Gaffer said sternly.

They heard a noise beyond the gate at the other end of the bridge.

"I think she's arrived," Mel said. Everyone started to move slowly forward, and then stopped, their eyes fixed on a school satchel, gripped by two hands, rising above the gate. At first they were gazing at its back, but then the satchel was reversed and turned upside down so its unbuckled flap fell open. They heard a muffled voice coming from inside.

"That's our brother," Lib said.

The satchel was shaken vigorously and the sounds coming from inside turned into desperate yells. Then a squirming body fell out and landed on the ground with a thud.

"Cherry," Lus cried. "Oh Cherry, you do look funny."

"He's turned into a clown," Mel exclaimed.

Cherry, dressed in a yellow blouse, baggy red trousers, a pointed green hat complete with bells, was struggling to get to his feet and walk in long, floppy slippers decorated with stars. He was almost in tears, but his mother was already doubled up with laughter, Ferriter was chuckling and Mel grinning. Gaffer having a quiet smile while his wife, pretending to be shocked, was trying hard not to smirk.

"He's made a habit off falling out of things," Josser said.

"Get me out of this gear," Cherry wailed.

"Oh Cherry," Lus said, "You do look pretty!"

Chapter 04
Confab

Josser and Mel were on the Gantry. Perched snugly against the warm casing of a winking signal light, and with their legs dangling in space, they were looking down on constant streams of cars, vans, and lorries — some of them huge — thundering in opposite directions. They were viewing the M99Z, known to them as the Great Roar. The din of the traffic was so great they had to shout at one another, but that they did not mind. Nor were they any longer afraid of walking or sitting on the Gantry, the terrifying way into their new home, which they called the Low Wood.

"Remember Auntie Bessiburger?" Mel shouted.

"What about her?"

"She was so scared she had to be blindfolded."

"And tied," Josser reminded his brother.

"That's right. Tied to Boff."

"And Slikky Bo," Josser added, and Mel chuckled.

"Won't forget that in a hurry," he said. "Boff asked what happens if they fall off and you told him to cut the rope quick. Slikky's never forgiven you."

"Well, he was useless then and he's still useless now. Auntie Bessiburger makes sossidges; he only makes speeches."

This conversation was diverted by the appearance below them of a car with flashing blue lights and a loud siren.

"Police," Mel explained.

"Is that why those things are all going slower?"

"Keeping within the speed limit."

The police car moved on, and, as its lights disappeared and the wail of its siren faded, the traffic below them speeded up.

"Does that mean the speed limit's been changed?" Josser asked.

"No. It means the police have gone."

They were silent for quite a long time.

"Daft," Josser said.

"What is?"

"Speed limits nobody keeps. Why not make those things so they can't go faster than the speed limit? Common sense."

"Do biggies have common sense?" Mel asked, and his brother considered.

"Reckon not," he finally said. "Beside that wouldn't be fair, would it? No one should have everything. Just look at the size of that lorry! It's big enough to carry all the food we'd need for a hundred years."

"I would settle for enough to get us through to harvesting," Mel said.

"We manage," Josser assured him. "We always do."

He sighed and said wistfully, "Though a sossidge sandwich and jar of bramble would not come amiss. Especially if it were two jars."

"Baldpatch says there are fruit trees beyond the bramble patches. Thinks there might have once been an orchard on our side of the fence."

"I'll settle for the brambles."

"Auntie Bessiburger's still got some."

"Some what?"

"Bramble wine. Matured. Really strong. Says she's keeping it for a special occasion, and she's not talking about your door."

They fell silent. The roar beneath their feet continued, and as the night sky darkened, the glare of the streaming headlights began to hurt.

"Time to go," Mel said.

Climbing down from the Gantry to the ground below required using a biggie-sized iron ladder which was not easy for him or his brother. When they reached the top of it and looked down at the ground which seemed very dark and distant, Mel remembered something.

"The first time we were here, I remember little Pipkin looking over this edge and saying, "Mr Gaffer, sir, it's a long way down from up. Do you remember what you said?"

"No," Josser replied.

"You should because it made Pipkin's mum very angry. I don't think she's even forgiven you. You patted her son on the head and said, 'Well, little boy, you can always close your eyes and jump."

"That was a joke!"

"Not all your jokes are funny. Shall we start down?"

The rungs of the biggie-sized ladder were far apart so Mel and Josser went down the side like climbing down a rope ladder. Half-way down they rested on a safety loop to catch their breath.

"I suppose Pipkin's mum is still mad at me?" Josser ventured.

"Probably, and she won't be the only one."

"Why? What have I done wrong now?"

"Caused Gaffer to call a confab. You'd forgotten. Hadn't you? Tomorrow."

"Oh no!" Josser wailed.

"You're an amnesiac," his brother told him.

"No, I'm not," Josser protested. "I'm not. I only forget

unimportant things. Now you've made me so worried I won't sleep."

They continued to climb down. When they were almost at the bottom and the noise of the Great Roar was so close it was deafening, Mel shouted, "You'll still snore."

"I don't snore," Josser yelled back.

"Yes, you do. You snore so loudly, babies as far away as the Pipes are kept awake. Pipkin's ma won't be the only one after your blood."

By then they were safely off the ladder and scuttling across the verge into the darkness beyond the glaring headlights. As they were dwarfs, who were far better at seeing in the dark than any biggies, they were soon striding down a zigzag path into the sheltering trees where the din of the Great Roar was diminished to a distant murmur.

"I won't sleep," Josser complained.

"You'll still snore," Mel told him.

If Josser slept, and his brother was sure that he did, because he heard the snores, there was one dwarf who certainly did not. Gaffer could not go to sleep because he had to think about the confab. Even though he had called this confab, Gaffer did not like confabs because, thanks to some dwarfs, most confabs ended up as shindigs, and he was afraid this one would do just that.

Confabs, which were held in the Dell, were supposed to be serious and orderly discussions about what to do next. That was the way all confabs began, but there were some dwarfs, and Gaffer could name all of them, who simply would not let confabs end as they began — seriously as well as orderly. They turned them into shindigs. Shindigs were fights which usually started between two or three argumentative dwarfs, but ended up with everyone trying to hit everyone else. There were those dwarfs, and Gaffer could certainly name all of them, who liked turning confabs into shindigs at the least excuse. There were even some who didn't need any excuse, and Gaffer knew all of them too well. They sat at the back. They were easily bored. They could be very argumentative, and Gaffer was never going to forget their names — Streaky, Limpet, and Josser.

When the last name flashed through Gaffer's tormented mind, he groaned so loudly he woke up Mrs. Gaffer, who promptly did what she promised whenever he became restless, and went to sleep in the other room. So Gaffer was left alone to have more dreadful thoughts if he was still awake, or suffer from a nightmare if he was not. So when he got up in the morning he was sure it was going to be a bad day, and the confab would most certainly become one of the worst shindigs ever because no one would have any idea how they could deal with that fearsome girl biggie known as PALS. Gaffer could not even eat his breakfast; he decided to have a headache.

Confabs were usually held late in the afternoon or early in the evening. The dwarfs would gather in the Dell, sitting in a semi-circle so Gaffer, sitting on a tump facing them, could easily speak to them all. But there were the trouble-makers, and Gaffer knew all of them, who always sat at the back, were easily bored, and rarely listened. When Josser strolled to the back and sat high up on the bank so he could swing his feet, Gaffer was not at all surprised.

Mel, on the other hand, came to sit in the semi-circle right under Gaffer's nose, because he was sensible like Boff, Tecky, and Clogs. The lady dwarfs, Gaffer always addressed them as 'our ladies' brought their knitting, except for Fancy, Slikky Bo's partner, and Miss Priss who carried parasols in case it rained. They also wore sunshades in case the sun was too bright for their delicate eyes. 'Our ladies' were never supposed to join in the shindigs, but some of them, firm believers in their more than equal rights, did. Lead by Auntie Bessiburger they would go into battle swinging their handbags and shouting 'Equality for us', while Miss Priss would close her eyes and cling to her parasol, and Fancy would wave her parasol and yell 'A big hug for the winner'.

Nurse Twiggs could be relied on to bring her emergency first aid box, and would treat most casualties, except for Josser. She allowed her friends to call her by her first name which was Thelma. Once Josser had tried to be familiar and had addressed her as 'Thermometer' which was a bad mistake; she would probably hit him with her first aid box.

Hazzi, Toga and Mrs. Toga, who were 'newcomers' because they had joined during the march, were sure to behave. There were two other newcomers, Nerdo, who would be no bother because he had never attended a confab, and Angus Macsnuffles, who might or might not come, which depended on whether he wanted to play his bagpipes. Playing bagpipes was only allowed close to the Great Roar where the painful noise was hidden by the greater din of the traffic.

When Ferriter arrived late, and went to sit at the back, next to Limpet, Gaffer feared the worst. Ferriter was still in a bad mood because Mrs. Gaffer had sent him to find jelly babies and he had come back with chewing gum. Or was it bubble gum? Mrs. Gaffer was bound to complain. Ferriter would stand up, protest and wave his fists about. He would probably hit Limpet by mistake. Limpet would also be kicked by Josser, by deliberate mistake, and that would be enough to start any shindig.

"Sorry," Ferriter said, and, taking off his hat, placed it on the bank so he could sit on it. Then he took a second hat out of his pocket and plonked it on his head so his bald patch would not get wet if it rained, folded his arms and said, "Ready. You can carry on."

Gaffer nodded to Yappo, who was supposed to keep order because he had a very sharp and clear voice, but sometimes forgot his duties and rushed into the shindig. Yappo banged on a battered tin drum and shouted, "Silence. Gaffer is speaking."

But before Gaffer could even open his mouth, Yappo was shouting, "Apologies. Apologies. Ma Bobble can't be with us. She has to look after her kids."

"That's a blessing," Josser shouted from the back. Auntie Bessiburger, who was twice his size, rounded on him.

"You'll be wanting sausages, will you not? And I want to listen. If I can't, you'll go without. Understand?"

Josser understood. Yappo shouted, "Gaffer will continue speaking."

So Gaffer was able to tell the gathering the sad tale of Cherry Bobble's kidnapping. Some found it amusing, particularly when Gaffer told them the boy simply refused to talk about how he was dunked in a jar of soapy water and thoroughly washed. They tried hard to look sorry when they heard how Cherry, dressed as a clown, had been returned by being dumped out of a school satchel.

Then Gaffer warned them about the child biggie known as PALS. She could see them, and that made her very dangerous. She was clever, scheming, venturesome, and even worse, she had a sense of humour. They would have to choose someone to deal with her when she returned. Someone who could act as her 'special friend'.

Old Gab, who had just woken up and didn't really know what Gaffer was talking about, asked, "Why is the biggie keeping us waiting for so long?"

"Because she can't meet us before. She's at a boarding school on the other side of the Great Roar," Mel explained. "Boarding school! What's that? Do the biggies send their kids away to be turned into planks?" Josser demanded.

"Boarding means the children live there," Mel explained.

"Sound like a good idea to me," Old Gab said. "Gets them out from under your feet."

"Stops them stealing your sossidges," Streaky added.

"Well," Josser said, "I'd certainly go for that." Mel groaned and closed his eyes; he knew what was going to happen.

As one, all the women turned to glare at his brother.

"This is all your fault," Mrs. Gaffer hissed. "You turned Cherry away."

"The poor little thing," said Miss Priss, pretending to cry into her dainty handkerchief.

"Time you were sorted out," added Auntie Bessiburger. They were about to advance on Josser, but Yappo banged his drum and diverted them.

"Proposal," he shouted. "Proposal from Slikky Bo. Slikky Bo speaks." Some groaned for when Slikky spoke, it was usually at great length. He stood, smoothed down his white hair, and cleared his throat.

"People," he began.

"Get on with it," Limpet yelled.

"People."

"You've just said that," Streaky pointed out.

"People!"

"Hear him out," Auntie Bessiburger warned.

"Thank you. People, it is our custom that those who make a mess are those who should sort it out."

"Hear! Hear!" the women said.

"I, therefore, nominate Josser as the 'special friend' who must deal with this biggie known as PALS."

"Those in favour?" Yappo shouted.

Up went every hand but one.

"The motion is carried," Yappo said.

"Objection!" Josser yelled.

"Against the rules. The vote has been taken," Yappo yelled back. "No further business, Gaffer."

"Then I declare this confab closed," Gaffer said and started to walk away.

"I want to complain," Mrs. Gaffer protested.

"My dear, I would never stop you complaining. Please go ahead. I'm off."

"I'm complaining about a certain forager," Mrs. Gaffer declared. "He is here, but I would never mention his name."

"She means you," Limpet told Ferriter. Mrs. Gaffer continued speaking.

"He was sent out to find jelly babies for our starving little children. What did he bring back? Bubble gum! Disgusting bubble gum. Bigger children, who should know better, chew it till their jaws are tired. What do they do next? They take the wad of gum out of their mouths and stick it anywhere. Disgusting."

"Shame," said all the ladies. "Shame!"

"My little one stuck his on my ball of knitting," Mrs. Mangle told them. "Now my hubby can't get his socks off." There was a great gasp of horror.

Throughout this tirade, Ferriter had been growing angrier and angrier. His face had turned red, beetroot, and then purple. He was incandescent with rage, or, as some old dwarfs would say 'his head was like two boiling kettles with steam coming out of both ears'. When Ferriter was in that state he shouted and waved his arms about wildly.

"That's downright unfair, Mrs. Gaffer. Downright unfair. I followed the rules your husband made. Don't comeback empty-handed, he said, and I never have. Never! I always come back with something. There were no jelly babies, but there was bubble gum. So I took that."

By the end of this speech, Ferriter was swinging his arms so wildly, one of his fists struck Josser in the eye. Josser, who was still coming to term with being voted the biggie's special friend, was knocked sideways into Limpet, who cannoned into Streaky. They both tumbled down the bank and bumped into Miss Priss, who shrieked. Josser staggered and reeled across the Dell, banging into Auntie Bessiburger. She screamed, "We're being attacked. Handbags." Whereupon all the ladies swung their handbags at Ferriter, Limpet, and Streaky, before flailing at everyone. The confab, which was over, had turned into a shindig.

When Mrs. Gaffer arrived home, her husband, complaining of a headache, was slumped in his armchair.

"Oh. I am sorry," said Mrs. Gaffer, who was not feeling at all sorry. "I will make you a cold compress."

She tore up an old newspaper, soaked the strips in cold water and vinegar, and plonked them on her husband's bald head, but not before she had sprinkled on some strong pepper to make his head feel on fire. She had not forgiven him for closing the confab before she could complain.

The newspaper which had been foraged by Ferriter, was a copy of the Times and dated 1938. Its headline was, 'Peace in Our Time'.

Chapter 05
The Special Friend.

Josser had decided he needed a badge. If he was going to be special, he must have a badge to show how important he had become. Ferriter, who was still upset after his telling off from Mrs. Gaffer for failing to find jelly babies, had been much more successful. He had come back with a round, shiny red badge which read 'PREFECT'.

Josser studied it and approved.

"That is definitely me," he declared. "Perfect".

"Well, you are not," Mel told him, "Besides that says 'Prefect'."

"What's a Prefect?"

"A child who tells other children what they should not do."

"I'm not a child," Josser protested." That word must be changed."

So the round, shiny red badge was handed over to Tecky who changed 'Prefect' to 'Speshul Fiend' which was the nearest he could get to Gaffer's choice of 'Special Friend.' When the badge was returned to Josser it was no longer shiny and not quite round. The red colour had been dulled and half the letters were in purple while the rest were blue.

"We ran out of purple paint," Tecky explained.

Nevertheless Josser would be able to wear his badge when they went to meet PALS for the second time.

"And remember the rules," Gaffer had repeated more than once. He had also handed over a small package with strict instructions it must be given to the biggie before any agreement was reached.

"What rules?" Josser asked his brother when they reached the Crooked Path.

"There's only one that really matters," Mel told him. "Tell her nothing. No names. Nothing about us. That kind of thing. She knows too much already."

Cherry had talked about being PALS' prisoner. He had admitted talking to the biggie, after shouting at her and calling her all the horrible names he could remember.

"Was she impressed?" Mel had asked.

"It was like talking to a big brick," Cherry had declared, but he had not revealed everything he had told her, beyond admitting Lib was his little sister, and he had another one called Lus, and he hoped neither would grow up to be like biggies. He said he had faced the biggie on the Crooked Path and told her not to frighten his little sisters. She had said nothing at the time, but dropped a large handkerchief over his head. While he was fighting to get free of the handkerchief she had picked him up and stuffed him in a pocket.

But he had also told them he had been fed on bits of toast and shreds of ham.

"Sound like you were treated like a guest," Josser said, thinking about the ham.

"I wasn't," Cherry had said. "I was a prisoner, kept in a jar and put on a shelf out of sight when she had visitors."

"Interesting," Mel had said. "She kept you hidden."

"She had her own room, and no one was allowed in. Even her mother and father had to knock and ask."

Cherry refused to talk about being dropped in a jar of soapy water and made to wash. Despite being asked several times, he insisted he had told the biggie absolutely nothing more.

"Be careful what you say," Mel warned.

"That's easy," Josser replied. "I'm going to let you do the talking. I'll just listen."

"Never," Mel told him. "For you, just listening would be like trying to do the impossible. Here she comes."

PALS was walking up the Crooked Path towards them, and she was so close they had to look up.

"You again," she said coldly.

"What's wrong with us?" Josser snapped.

"I told you," Mel said, giving him a nudge. Josser nudged him back.

"You definitely are brothers," PALS said.

"How did you guess? Ah! I know. We both have big red noses." Josser was already getting angry.

"I give up," Mel said.

"You argue," PALS told them. "I have a brother and he tries to argue with me, but I've stopped him."

"How?" Mel asked. "If it isn't a secret, I would like to know."

"No secret, and it's very simple. I scream at him. Would you like to hear me scream?" Both dwarfs looked up at her, and decided they would not.

"No, thank you," Mel said.

"Good. We will walk up to the bench. We can sit down and you can listen to my terms. It won't take long, and then you can go away while I talk to Cherry's little sisters."

She strode on, leaving Josser and Mel to gape at one another. Then they scuttled after her.

"You can't do that," Mel shouted. "Nothing has been agreed."

"It has. Cherry agreed I could meet his sisters. By the way, how is he? Is he still clean? He was such a dreadful mess."

She sat down on the bench, and waited for them to clamber on the other end, and stand facing her.

"We have rules," Josser tried.

"Good. I hope you keep them."

"Will you?"

"If you have rules for me, just tell me them. I might agree."

"We must know when you are coming here, and you must agree one of us goes with you, wherever you go."

"That's easy. Which one? Do I have a choice?"

The dwarfs looked at each other. Gaffer had made dealing with the biggie sound easy, but this biggie kept on asking awkward questions. Before they could make up their minds, PALS was standing up.

"Here come Lib and Lus," she said. "While you're deciding, I'm going to talk to them." She walked away as the sisters approached, with Cherry trailing behind.

"This is hopeless!" Josser shouted, and stamped his foot.

"Not quite," Mel said. "Let them chat. Be friendly. I'll have a quiet word with Cherry. Do what you said you would. Just listen."

"They're going to show her how to play 'hops'," Cherry said when he reached the bench.

"Friends already," Mel said thoughtfully as they watched the girls walk back down the path. Lus was leading the way because she was so eager to show her new friend the smooth bit of the path which was the best place for playing hops.

"You have some explaining to do," Josser told Cherry sternly. He looked very sheepish.

"Well, I couldn't help it, could I?" he said defensively. "I was her prisoner."

"Did she torture you?" Josser asked. "Did she threaten to tear you limb from limb, as I am about to?"

"It wasn't like that! I don't know. She just talked and talked. Kept asking questions."

"Asked if you had brothers and sisters," Mel prompted.

"Yes."

"Asked where you lived?"

"Yes."

"What did you tell her?"

"Well. Not much. Only that we lived in a boot. But it wasn't a real boot, because it came from a fancy shop for ladies."

"Then she asked you how you knew that?"

"That's right!" Cherry was so surprised he could not prevent himself from saying more. Too much more.

"So I said Slikky Bo told me, 'cos he knows about such things."

"Slikky Bo," Mel said, with a shake of his head.

"Did I say something wrong?" Cherry asked.

"Blabbermouth," Josser told him. He raised his hands and groaned. "We're lost. That biggie is going to know everything. There won't be any deal. Gaffer will be mad at us and she'll trample us into the dust."

"Not yet," Mel said thoughtfully. "Not yet, unless Cherry has said something absolutely silly."

"Would I do that?" the boy asked.

"Yes," he was firmly told.

"We have to talk to her," Mel said.

"As we agreed?" his brother asked. "You talk and I listen?"

"Let's start that way," Mel suggested, "And you be ready to do your disappearing act."

48

"Can he do that?" Cherry was eager to know.

"And I can make nosys disappear — permanently," Josser growled.

So they went down the Crooked Path to where the girls were playing happily.

Lus had explained how the game of hops required the drawing of squares and circles no bigger than the size of your foot, and then jumping from one shape to the other. Then she had tried to draw a square the size of PALS foot and had run out of chalk halfway through. PALS had used a sharp stone to scratch a square on the path.

"We'll never rub that out," Josser complained. The girls took no notice.

"You can call me Penny," PALS told the sisters.

"Is Penny your real name?" Lib asked.

"No. My real name is Penelope Arabella Leamington Spa, and I hate it."

"That's not a name," Lus said. "It's a sentence."

"In more ways than one," Penny said philosophically.

"We'll settle for Penny," Lib said. "Can we get on with the game? You go first."

So Penny hopped first, obeying the rule that you must always hop from one shape to a different shape until you had hopped through all the shapes at least once. When she had finished successfully her new friends clapped and cheered.

"Now it's our go," Lib said, and when the two little sisters had finished just as successfully, Penny applauded and said, "We've all won. What shall we do next?"

"Oh, the game isn't over yet," Lib told her. "Now it's time for round two."

"What's that?" Penny asked. Lus wanted to ask the same

49

question because she had never heard of a round two, but she kept quiet because she knew her sister was making it up so they would win.

"Well," Lib began, "We have to hop through your shapes, and you have to hop through ours."

"You'll never do that. My shapes are too far apart!" Penny pointed out.

"Well," Lib went on, "There is another rule for if you're little. Isn't there, Lus?"

Lus nodded franticly, hoping she would not be asked.

"What is it?" Penny asked.

"Running hops," Lib said quickly. "If you are little you are allowed to run out of one shape, but you must hop into the next. Only if you are little. Watch." Before Penny could disagree, Lib was on her way, running and then hopping.

Lus, who quickly caught on to her sister's thinking, shouted 'Yeah!' before following her example. When they had both completed their round two successfully, they both turned and looked up at their new friend.

"Your turn," Lib said, "And there's a special rule for biggies. No socks and shoes."

It was something she had just thought up because she wanted to see the biggie's toes. Lus, who wanted to be friends with the biggie, did not know what she would do if the biggie refused. If Penny walked away Lus might never see her again. But if Lus took the biggie's side and pleaded with Lib to drop her silly rule, her sister might be very cross and that would mean a pillow bashing when they went to bed. It was all too complicated.

But, at that very moment, Josser decided he had watched enough. He coughed.

"Oh. Hello," Penny said brightly, "You haven't come back

with your army. Where are they?"

Cherry gulped, and turned to run away. Josser gripped him by the arm.

"He hasn't told you?" Penny went on. "He threatened me. He said if I didn't let him go you would come after me with hundreds of archers, and I would have more arrows sticking in me than his mother's pin cushion has pins. What do you think of that?"

"I think our children should go home," Mel said. "Go on, Cherry, take your sisters home. Disappear!" They watched Cherry drag his very reluctant sisters away. Lus managed to say a rather tearful 'Bye' while her sister waved and shouted 'We won'.

"Now we can talk seriously," Mel went on, "About rules. Josser has something to give you. Josser! Oh! He's done it again."

"Done what?" Penny asked.

"Disappeared. We can all do it. It's a very good way of dealing with people we don't want to meet. Disappear." Mel looked up at Penny and smiled.

"Can you see him anywhere? No. He is so good at disappearing. Go on. Look around. Wherever you look, he won't be there." Penny refused to look. She glared down at Mel.

"I think you're trying to tell me something," she said.

"He is," Josser said, and she almost jumped for there he was, standing by his brother.

"We will all disappear," Josser went on. "You will come looking and we just won't be here, there or anywhere to be seen." "No army," Mel added, "but where is yours?"

"Mine? I don't understand," Penny protested.

"All those skateboarding friends you would bring whizzing

through our woods."

"Oh! Them." Penny blushed and seemed to be struggling to find an answer. Then she changed the subject and became indignant.

"This isn't your property. It's a designated area for wild life." Josser was not to be diverted.

"What do you think we are? We're alive and we're getting wilder by the minute."

Mel added to the pressure.

"And you haven't got any skateboarding friends. You haven't got any friends at all. Have you?"

It was Penny's turn to cry, and although she tried her hardest not to, a tear trickled down one cheek. The dwarfs watched in silence until she hurriedly tried to wipe her tear away, and nodded.

"Good," Josser said. "Now we can talk."

So they returned to the bench and sat down. Penny meekly agreed to the rules, though with her fingers crossed behind her back, and Josser promised she could meet all the children, but only if they wanted to meet her. Then he handed her the package and said, "There have to be some very strict rules. Please open this." Inside was the clown's costume, cleaned, spotless, ironed and neatly folded.

"But I meant this to be a gift!" Penny exclaimed.

"No gifts," Mel said. "If you give to one, you must give to all, and if you went on giving that would make us dependent on a biggie which would never do."

"We would end up being a tourist attraction, and someone would carry us away to a circus," Josser added.

"Oh! But no one can come in here. This is private."

"No, it isn't," Josser argued. "Private is beyond the high

fence and there are notices in big red letters. We never go there."

"That's different," Penny said. "That's dangerous because there's an abandoned mine in there."

"Abandoned mine," Josser exclaimed, "that would suit the Bats down — Ow!"

He started hopping around and clutching at one leg.

Penny stared at Mel.

"Did I just see you kick your brother?" she asked.

"No," Mel said, trying to sound innocent, "I was just waggling my foot to get rid of the cramps and he bumped into it."

Then they had to wait for Josser to get over his accident, and forgot all about what they were saying just before it happened.

"You asked me which one I should choose. Remember?" Penny said.

"Him," Josser said pointing at his brother.

"No." Penny said firmly. "No. Cherry said you are always the one to start an argument." She pointed at Josser, her finger almost touching his nose, as she added, "You. I do enjoy arguing."

"When are you coming again?" asked Mel, and Penny beamed.

"You mean I can?"

"Not tomorrow," Josser said hurriedly, "I must get on with my house."

"I would like to, but I can't. I'm back at school for a whole month."

"Oh. Ooh!" Josser said, for his brother kicked him again before he could say 'good'.

"Oh dear. That is a pity," he finally said.

So everything was agreed and they could all go home feeling

pleased because they had all got what they wanted.

"What will we tell Gaffer?" Mel asked.

"You can tell him," Josser said, "Remember we did agree you would do all the talking."

"What if he doesn't like it?"

"Then I will blame you," Josser said, and, after a sigh, added, "Today has been a very hard day. Tomorrow I might come down to the stream and watch you fish, or I might think about killing Cherry. Saying I always argue."

"You do, and you say too much. You told the biggie you were going to work on your house," Mel protested.

"Not before I get over my injuries. Besides I will be thinking hard, and hard thinking is just as tiring as working. What colour will I paint my door? Bright yellow or deep purple?"

Chapter 06
The Hidden Garden

They did not go fishing. When tomorrow came and promptly turned into today, which it always did, the rain also came. The rain stayed for three whole days. Sometimes the brothers were very wet and other times they were just damp, but they were becoming grumpier with each other.

Their grumpiness began because the house under the tree was not quite ready; it had no door. They were still having to sleep in their tent which leaked and dripped raindrops on their heads. When they tried sleeping in the house their toes got wet because the rain formed puddles on the floor; there was no door to stop it coming in.

"If you'd let Boff make your door, my feet wouldn't be wet," Mel complained, pointing to a very wet big toe poking through a hole in one sock.

"Boff is not going to make my door," his brother shouted. "I'm going to make it, and it's going to be very special."

Their mood became worse on the third morning when all they had left to eat was few crusts of very stale bread.

"I'll make toast," Josser offered. "The wood is dry, and we can light a fire in my new fireplace." But he couldn't because his new fireplace was standing in its own pool of water. He had forgotten to cap his chimney pot. Even though Mel said absolutely nothing, Josser shouted at him.

"I know what you're thinking," he shouted.

"I'm so glad you can read my mind," Mel shouted back.

"Saves me wasting my breath." So they ate the bread which was still very stale, and glowered at each other.

When the afternoon came the rain almost stopped and the sun tried to shine.

"Time to go fishing," Mel said.

"But will you catch anything?" his brother asked. Mel ignored the question, until he was standing as near to the stream as he dared.

"The answer is no," he said. The stream had become a torrent of turbulent brown water carrying with it broken twigs and leaves.

"Go hungry then," Josser said.

"Don't we all? Will we last out till our own crops are ready?"

"Simple answer to that," Josser said. "We must." Mel stared at the rushing waters.

"Perhaps tomorrow," he said and then sighed. "I suppose we go home now, and you think beautiful thoughts about your door."

"Shut up," Josser said.

They were on the edge of another argument, but before Mel could answer back, they saw two figures struggling along the bank of the stream. One, on her feet, was pulling and tugging at the other who was sagging on his knees.

"That's Tiddy Mangle," Mel said.

"Who is she dragging?" Josser asked, and they both waved.

Tiddy saw them, let go of the person she was pulling to wave back. He fell flat on his face, right into the mud.

"Help," Tiddy cried, and stooped over to haul her friend to his feet.

"It's Cherry," Mel said.

"Falling down instead of out," Josser said. "That makes a change."

"What happened?" Mel asked when they reached the couple.

"What? Oh. Yes. Cherry slipped on a stone, and fell in the stream. He's a complete mess." Tiddy said hurriedly as if she were making up a story as she spoke.

Cherry, who was coated with mud, mumbled, "Ma will kill me."

"Save someone a job," Josser said, and Tiddy glared at him.

"You can't be nice to anyone, can you? No wonder Ma hasn't forgiven you."

"Help Cherry home," Mel said. The children staggered on while Josser gaped.

"What was all that about?" he asked.

"Another of your bad jokes," Mel told him.

"Bad jokes. What bad joke? I don't remember."

"Years ago, when we were on the march. Tiddy was still a baby in her cradle. You looked down at her and said, "You are a nice little thing. Can I have a bite?""

"Well, I was feeling hungry," Josser protested. "We all were."

"Mrs Mangle hit you," Mel went on. "She also hit Streaky because he laughed, but he's apologised so she's forgiven him."

"So now I should apologise for cracking a joke!"

"Bad joke," Mel said, and, noticing a very little figure trudging towards them, added, "Hello. Who's coming our way now?"

Walking out of the sun-warmed mist was a chubby toddler with a very puzzled look on his face.

"Foggy," Mel said, and he was not talking about the weather. He was identifying the little child who always wore a slight frown as if he didn't know where he was or why. Consequently everyone called him 'Foggy'.

"Extraordinary!" Mel added, not because Foggy was wet up to the waist and streaked with as much mud as Cherry, but because he was clutching a carrot almost as big as himself.

"What have you got there?" Mel asked.

Foggy looked up at him, hugged the carrot tightly and said, "It's mine. You can't have it." His frown became a very determine scowl. "Not yours," he declared.

"Stop!" Josser shouted, not at Foggy, but at Tiddy and Cherry, who were now trying to run away. "Back here now!" They turned, look at each other, shrugged unhappily, and obeyed.

"You can't have my carrot," Foggy was telling Mel again, "It's all mine, but you can have a little onion because Snips grows them even though she doesn't like them. Got to go home now." Before Mel could stop him, Foggy was toddling on.

"Foggy, at least tell me where you got that carrot," Mel pleaded.

"Must get home. Eat my carrot," Foggy, still moving, mumbled. Then he stopped, faced Mel and said, "That's easy. Mrs. Intpot. Ask Snips. That's where she gets onions."

"Oh, no. We're done for now," Cherry wailed.

It had become such a mysterious matter, Josser and Mel, in agreement for once, decided it would have to be solved by Gaffer. Tiddy and Cherry, both looking extremely guilty, had refused to say anything more until they faced Gaffer, which would be after they faced their mothers which would be bad enough. Tiddy muttered darkly about putting the blame on Josser.

"I don't think your mother would swallow that," Mel warned, and Tiddy shrugged.

"Well, I only went along to help," she said, and stomped off.

Josser and Mel went home, brewed nettle tea which they had to drink unsweetened, and shared just one of their few remaining oatcakes.

"At least the sun is shining," Mel said.

"Brilliant," Josser said, meaning exactly the opposite.

"Doesn't anything even cheer you up? Just a little bit?"

"A big bite of that carrot would have cheered me up," Josser said. Just before he went to sleep, he said to himself gloomily, "First thing in the morning, Pipkin would be banging on my door, if I had one."

Josser was right, but Pipkin arrived late, and looking very nervous.

"You don't have to tell us," Josser said. "There is an emergency, and Gaffer wants us to sort it out."

"Something like that, I suppose," Pipkin mumbled.

"What kind of emergency?" Mel asked.

"Oh. I don't know. I must hurry. I have to fetch Boff." Mel watch him scurry away.

"That lad does know something," he said.

When they arrived at Gaffer's there was a crowd of children, all of them little, clustered round the door.

"Looks as if jelly babies have arrived," Josser said.

"If that were so, they would be smiling," Mel pointed out.

The children were looking unhappy. Some of them, including Foggy, looked as though they were about to cry. Gaffer appeared in the doorway and told them to sit down and be very quiet. They obeyed. Gaffer turned to Josser and Mel.

"Thieves," he explained. "They've all confessed to stealing vegetables from old Mrs. Intpot's garden. Who is Mrs. Intpot?"

"Foggy knows," Mel said.

Hearing that, Foggy began to cry, and because he cried, all the other children had to cry too. Their wailing was deafening. Miss Priss rushed out, clapped her hands and said "Oh. Please, children, do try to be quiet." Their wailing became a howl, and then she too was in tears. Just as the noise was reaching an intolerable crescendo, Boff arrived and bellowed, "Shut up!" There was immediate silence.

"I think they should all go home," Josser suggested. No one waited for Gaffer to give the order. Before he could open his mouth all the little children were gone, and Miss Priss was not long in following them, with her hands over her ears because Boff's bellow had deafened her.

"It's such a mess," Gaffer said as he sat down on bench outside his house.

"What is?" Josser asked.

"All those children stealing vegetables. Who's got vegetables? From where?"

He was very flustered.

"Well, I'm not much in favour of children myself," Josser said, "but they do like to eat, and they're only doing what we've had to do for years."

"The foragers do that now," Gaffer said. "I thought we'd agreed."

"Foragers. Useless," Mrs Gaffer, who had joined the meeting as she always did, said. "And all those children owned up."

"Maybe not all," Mel said. "I can think of one who wasn't even here."

"What! Are you telling me we haven't heard everything? We must investigate. You must investigate!"

Gaffer was on his feet and heading indoors.

"Don't let me delay you. You must investigate immediately. Is there any tea in the pot?"

"He sent for me!" Boff exclaimed. "Why?"

"To investigate!" Gaffer shouted, but remained out of sight.

Miss Priss reappeared, holding a wide-eyed toddler by his arm.

"Chatty will tell you. Won't you, Chatty?" she said, and Chatty nodded.

"There, you see," Miss Priss went on. "They will talk to you if you're nice to them. Shouting at them is so useless, it makes me want to cry." She put a handkerchief to her eyes.

"You poor dear," Mrs Gaffer said. "Come with me. We could both do with a nice cup of tea."

"So could I," shouted Gaffer, and they heard his angry rattle of an empty teapot.

"What's your name?" Mel asked the toddler.

"Chatty."

"That's a useless question," Josser protested. "We all know his name."

"Being friendly," Mel explained. "Putting him at ease. Do you like carrots?" Chatty nodded and said, "And pods. I likes pods best."

"There," Mel said, "he's talking already. Who gives you pods, Chatty?"

"Dunno."

"He's stopped talking," Josser said.

"Perhaps I asked the wrong question," Mel said, and tried again.

"Where do you get the pods?"

"Dunno."

"Did Foggy give you them?"

"Dunno."

"Can I go now?" Pipkin asked. "You don't seem to need me."

"You stay right where you are?" Mel told him firmly.

"Let Dunno go," Josser said, "his lips are sealed."

When the toddler reached a safe distance, he turned, said, "Me name's not Dunno," stuck out his tongue, made a rude noise and ran off.

"Now what?" Boff asked.

"Round up Tiddy and Cherry. Bring them down to where the rill meets the stream. They're going to show us where Mrs. Intpot grows her vegetables. "

"I'll go with him," Pipkin volunteered.

"No, you won't," Mel said sharply. "You're coming with us. Take us to see that missing child, Snips."

"Why is she called Snips?" Josser asked.

"When she was very little, she took her ma's scissors and cut off her hair. She wanted to look like daddy. He's bald."

"I hope she's come to her senses," Josser said.

Snips was in her own garden, making sure all her wooden peg dollies were eating up their breakfasts. It was such an important ritual she made them go through it three times every day. As she simply refused to interrupt this routine, Josser and Mel had to crawl along guttering under some nettles to reach her garden where her dollies, propped up against a miscellany of chipped plant pots, were waiting to be fed.

Each pot, standing in its own puddle, was a riot of spring onions, lettuce, sweet peas, and many other flowers. Snips, her surviving tufts of hair tied back with bows of ribbon, was armed with her mother's scissors. She was cutting leaves and sprouts off her plants before feeding the bits to her dollies; they did not seem very interested.

"Hello," she said.

"Where did you get all those pots?" Mel asked.

"Daddy dug them up. I helped him."

62

Josser, who had taken a close look into one pot said, "This isn't ordinary soil. This is compost."

"Limpet gives me that. He's my friend."

"He must be," Josser said because he was amazed. Limpet got his name because he never parted with anything.

"Do your dollies eat the flowers?" was his next question. Snips stared at him.

"Of course they don't. Flowers are for looking at. You are silly."

"Over to you," Josser told his brother.

"Is Foggy your friend?"

"I like Foggy," Snips said, "and we can both get through the hedge."

"And pull carrots," Mel suggested.

"Carrots fall off Thuggydear's barrow. Foggy just picks them up."

"Like the onions."

"No. They fall off a tin roof. I roll them through the hedge."

"Then what happens to them, Snips?"

"I bring them home and look after them. Do you want to see?"

"Yes please."

Snips pointed to a half-covered wicker basket. "In there," she said.

Josser looked and nodded.

"Enough to make soup for all of us," he said. Mel knew he had to ask the right question, which was not about onion soup.

"Snips, who else is there when you go through the hedge?"

"No one else goes through hedge. I go. Foggy goes, and Tiddy and Cherry aren't there because Mrs Intpot is chasing them."

"What about Pipkin? Is he ever there?"

"Oh, no. Pipkin is always up a tree."

"I want you to show me a tree," Mel told Pipkin when they were on their way again and very near to where the rill flowed into the stream.

"Well, there are lots of trees," Pipkin said nervously.

"And then I want you show me where you get through the fence," Mel went on.

"Get through the fence! I don't get through the fence. No one gets through that fence." Then realising he had said too much, Pipkin went red in the face, and said "Oops" just as Tiddy and Cherry, shadowed by Boff, arrived.

Tiddy took one look at Pipkin's guilty face and said, "I knew it. Blown our secret. My mum was right about men. You're all rude and useless."

"Can you climb the right tree?" Josser asked her.

"You dummy!" Tiddy yelled, and tried to get at Pipkin. Boff held her back.

"I'll show you," Pipkin said as he backed away.

"Ma will kill me for sure," Cherry said.

"With my help," Tiddy told him.

Then they watched in silence while Pipkin pointed to a tree overhanging both the stream and the rill, and Mel climbed it. It seemed an age before he came down, dusted his hands and said, "Yes, there is a garden, and it's full of vegetables."

Chapter 07
Aunt Sally's

"They didn't break the rules," Josser said firmly. "They went under the fence not through it. Thanks to Mastermind here. He thought it all out." Pipkin, who was standing at the back of the room, blushed and hoped no one would look at him. He was only present because Gaffer might need a messenger, but he did not want to be asked too many questions about his part in the thieving. Josser, however, was in no mood to let him off lightly, and went on to tell the meeting that Pipkin had happened to see the garden because he was high up in a tree. He had then crept under the wire followed by Snips who wanted to pick flowers. She had spotted the onion lying in the bed of the stream and thought she would take it home because it was lost and needed looking after.

Josser looked directly at Pipkin and went on, "Mastermind here told Snips the onion belonged in a garden on the other side of the hedge they were looking at, and she volunteered to put it back. Before he could stop her, she was crawling through the hedge trying to drag the onion with her. Then she gave up and let the onion roll back into stream. She didn't come back with it, but appeared later to tell Mastermind she had seen a carrot, and Foggy liked carrots. He would look after it." By then all eyes were on Pipkin and he was wishing the ground would open and swallow him up.

"There is a lot I don't understand," Gaffer said. "You say they were walking along the bed of the stream. How could they?

Surely it's far too deep."

"Especially for little children," Mrs Mangle added. She had invited herself to the meeting because Tiddy had cried her eyes out. That awful Josser had been overheard telling everyone that her darling Tiddy had only cried because Boff had prevented her from choking Cherry and pounding Pipkin into dust.

Mel tried to explain.

"The garden is on an island in the middle of the stream. The part the children walked up is usually quite shallow, and little ones could creep under the fence. The heavy rain washed away the bank and made getting under much easier."

"I think we need a map. It's much easier if we can see what we're talking about," Mrs Gaffer said. She was there because no one had found a way of keeping her out of any meeting.

"I can get one," Pipkin shouted. "From Nerdo. He'll make one."

"Will that take long?"

"No. I'll run all the way there and back." Before anyone could stop him, Pipkin was out of the door and running as fast as he could.

"Time for a cup of tea," Gaffer said.

"I knew you'd say that," Mrs. Gaffer told him.

"Nerdo can do something useful!" Boff exclaimed. He sounded as if he couldn't believe it. Boff was at the meeting because Gaffer had chosen him to be an investigator, though he had not done any investigating. He was quite content to leave that to Josser and Mel who were more used to getting into trouble than he was.

"I like making things," he would often say. "Much better than arguing."

There was time for Gaffer to have a second cup of tea before

Pipkin returned with a map that explained everything. It impressed Mel because, on paper, the island looked almost the same shape as the one he had looked down on from the tree.

"Nerdo drew that!" Boff exclaimed.

"No," Pipkin replied, "he copied it. Google drew it."

"Goggle! Who's Goggle? Has Nerdo got a lodger?" Josser asked.

"Don't answer," Mel pleaded. "Goggle, go cart, or Google. The name doesn't matter. The map's fine. Can we get on with things?"

"Only if you explain it," Mrs Gaffer urged him.

So Mel told how he and Josser had walked along the shallow stream until it joined the deep stream, and had found themselves standing beside a footbridge and looking up at a very high gate. Above the gate was a notice which read 'Aunt Sally's Vegetable and Fruit Garden. Only the Best. Cash Preferred. Credit given to Special Customers ONLY. No deal too small. Deposit required. Beware of the Dog.'

"What does all that mean?" Boff asked.

"We can buy beans," Josser told him.

"And lots of other things," Mel added.

"Should we be punishing Pipkin? He seems to have discovered a source of food," Gaffer mused.

"We are making him be useful. Maybe we might even forgive him," Josser conceded.

The meeting considered the list, handing it from one to another and becoming very excited about foods such as oatmeal, carrots and pods.

"Are we special customers?" Mrs Gaffer asked, and that silenced them because no one believed they could be special.

"Have we got any bits?" Mrs Mangle asked.

"A few," Gaffer admitted. "I've been keeping them for a rainy day."

"It's arrived," Josser said.

"What! Is it raining again? I hadn't noticed," Boff said. No one bothered to answer.

"How many bits?" Mel asked.

Mrs. Gaffer went to look for Gaffer's second-best purse because he could never find anything straightaway even if it were right under his nose.

"Time for another cup," Boff hinted and everyone glared at him.

The purse was discovered in the bottom of Mrs. Gaffer's knitting basket.

"I wondered where you'd put it this time," Gaffer said when she plonked it on the table.

"Looks rather empty," Boff said, and he was right. When they tipped the coins on to the table there were only nine.

"Enough to buy a cabbage," Josser said.

Gaffer pushed the coins towards him and said, "I'm sure you can do much better than that."

"Why us?" Josser asked as the brothers trudged home.

"I thought Gaffer said you," Mel pointed out. "He didn't name me."

"You're not going to leave me to deal with this Mrs. Intpot on my own!" Josser protested. "We are brothers and we should do things together."

"If that means you're expecting me to help you make your door, you can think again," Mel said, "And we don't know if Mrs. Intpot is Aunt Sally."

When Pipkin had tried to explain that Mrs. Intpot was the

name the little children had given to a person they had never seen, the meeting had become confused and disorderly.

"They just hear her screeching at Tiddy and Cherry who are banging on the gate and calling her rude names," he had explained.

"My Tiddy would never do that!" Mrs Mangle had protested.

"What words did they hear?" Gaffer had asked.

"I'll put ye in t'pot," Pipkin had replied.

"I would never threaten little children like that," Mrs Gaffer said.

"I know someone who would," Mrs. Mangle had muttered darkly.

"Intpot or Aunt Sally, I'm sure Josser will know how to deal with the lady," Gaffer had said, putting an end to any argument which might quickly turn into a shindig, before reminding them that Auntie Bessiburger's food bank was almost empty.

"But then, I might come along, just to see what happens," Mel said. "When do we go?"

"Right now," Josser replied. "We might come home with something to eat for supper."

He shook the purse making whatever was inside clink.

"That looks quite full and sounds like it holds more than nine bits," Mel said thoughtfully.

"Oh, good," his brother said. Only their boots got wet as they trudged up the shallow stream after ducking under the fence. As they walked towards the gate to the garden, they looked for the hole in the hedge through which Snips and Foggy had crawled but could not spot it. Then they came to the narrow footbridge and the high garden gate. Mel stared up at the notice.

"I don't like that bit about the dog," he said.

"Maybe there isn't one. Mrs. Intpot put up the notice to scare off people," Josser suggested, but then they both heard a very doggy and savage snarl.

"That didn't sound like a notice to me," Mel said. They both stared up at the gate.

"Tiddy said she had to scrabble up, cling on with one hand while she waved the other and yelled," he went on.

"What did Cherry do?"

"He said he kicked a hole in the gate." They continued to stare at the gate. It seemed undamaged.

"Cherry does exaggerate," Josser said, and then he banged as hard as he could on the gate.

"Ma, there's someone bashing our gate."

"If its them Bat brats again, set Boris on them, Thuggydear."

"I don't think it's them, Ma. These ain't kicking or saying nasty things."

They heard a sigh, then, "Wait a minute', followed by the crunch of big feet on gravel.

"Who be there?" a shrill voice screeched.

"Customers," Josser shouted.

"Ooh! Customers! How nice! Thuggydear, put Boris on his chain, but don't feed him. He bites better when he's hungry."

They heard the scrape of bolts being drawn back, before the gate was slowly opened. Standing before them was a lady dressed in a flowing black gown festooned with many necklaces, chains, and bangles. On her feet she wore huge bright yellow slippers decorated with dots of all colours. Her red hair stuck out in all directions from under a floppy hat the same colour as her slippers. Looming behind her was her son, Thuggydear. He had the same staring eyes and red hair as his mother, but while her hair spread in all directions, his was plastered down with a very shiny hair cream, making his head look like an upside-down Easter egg half-wrapped in orange foil.

"Customers," Mrs Intpot crooned, her eyes fixed on the purse Josser was holding.

"Have we come to spend lots of lovely bits?" she asked sweetly.

"Thinking about it," Josser said.

"Good! We have a customer who thinks, Thuggydear. Is your lovely purse cram packed with lots of lovely little bits?" She stretched out a hand in an effort to touch the purse, but Josser was too quick and moved the purse out of her reach. He shook it making the contents jingle.

"Ooh!" Mrs Intpot said.

"Might come back and spend a lot," Josser said.

"Why not do it today? Doing things today is always better than leaving them till tomorrow," Mrs. Intpot urged.

"That is what I always say, but I've got to see what you've got and tell others. Am I speaking to Aunt Sally?"

Mrs. Intpot shrieked with laughter.

"A customer with a sense of humour. I think I'm going to like you, my dear new friend," Mrs. Intpot spread her arms wide. "We got the lot. Fresh and dried veggies, fruits, oatmeal and fine flour. The absolute lot. See for yourself. As for Aunt Sally, she's our frightener and she's over there."

Mrs Intpot pointed to a towering scarecrow with a turnip head, corks for eyes, cabbage leaves for ears, and hands made from old garden trowels. It was propped against a water-wheel driven by bicycle pedals.

"As we are now friends, you can call me Prunella. I will show you round. Follow me. Thuggydear, our lovely plants need a drink." Her son leaped on the bicycle, pedalled furiously making the waterwheel spin and hurl water in all directions. As Mel and Josser followed Prunella they were drenched, and eyed by the growling Boris who sounded suspicious. Mrs Intpot capered backwards and forwards, trying to get the purse into her grasp.

"Excellent," Josser said after he had looked into the shed and seen the sacks of onions, beans, and oatmeal. "I will definitely return, but now I would like to buy enough for a feast. Just enough for myself and my friends." He put his hand in his purse and took out a handful of bits which he carefully counted. "There," he said, "eight bits. Enough for a feast." Prunella tried hard to hide her disappointment.

"You don't have many friends, do you?" she hinted.

"You can say that again," Mel added quietly, because he was thinking his brother had gone completely mad.

"We never guzzle. We want to keep our slim and youthful figures." Mel almost choked; his brother was going just too far. Prunella was looking puzzled. The dog was on his feet and pulling against his chain.

"For eight bits," Prunella muttered.

"Few carrots, onions and stuff like that," Josser said airily, "Perhaps a bag of oatmeal. Good food for slimmers, oatmeal."

"Thuggydear, bring a couple of carrots, an onion, not one of the large, a handful of pods, and a scoop of oatmeal," Mrs. Intpot ordered. Her son obeyed, placing the few vegetables in a basket.

"Is that all?" Josser asked. Mrs. Intpot's smile disappeared.

"We are not a charity," she said coldly.

"But we are new customers," Josser said, "Surely, you offer first time customers a discount?" Then he began to pick up his bits, dropping them back into his purse, one by one.

Prunella watched in silence, until she could no longer bear

the sight of bits disappearing into a purse.

"Thuggydear fetch one of those cabbages we were going to put on the heap."

"That is so kind," Josser said a big smile, as he handed over the bits. "Excellent. I'm sure we'll be back with a big order in a few days." He shook his purse under Prunella's nose.

"Plenty more where these came from."

"I hate cabbage," Mel complained. They were safely back on their side of the fence and trudging along the bank of the stream.

"That makes two of us," Josser said.

"But I'm the one carrying it," Mel protested. Josser was carrying the other vegetables and the oatmeal in an old sack which Prunella said was a free gift because they were such good customers.

"And what about this big order?" he went on. "How are you going to pay for that? With buttons?"

"That's a thought," Josser said.

Then they met Cherry and Nerdo. Cherry said he was taking his friend for a walk in the fresh air and out of his stuffy pad. Nerdo shivered and said he supposed he would be all right though he did not much like the cold smell of fresh.

"How can you have a cold smell?" Josser asked.

"Hey, man, have you no soul?" Nerdo asked in return. "Have you no poetry? No dreams?"

"Oh, I have dreams," Josser told him. "Mostly about frying sausages."

Cherry hurriedly said, "Time we moved on."

"Yeah," Nerdo drawled. "Back to the nice warm smells of my pad." Then he looked directly at Josser and went on, "Hey, man, you're so square you're cubed."

Then he and Cherry walked on, leaving Josser almost speechless, but not quite.

"Where did we find him?" he asked. "I didn't notice him when we were first on the march."

"He wasn't," Mel replied. "He appeared after we came out of the Navs' tunnel. Said he wanted a change of scenery. Gaffer said he could join us as long as he made himself useful, and he did."

"How?" Josser wanted to know.

"By carrying toddlers." Josser was so disgusted he grumbled all the way home.

Chapter 08
The Big Deal

"You were robbed," Mrs. Gaffer said.

"This cabbage is the worst ever," Auntie Bessiburger added. Josser glowered.

"You weren't there," he said.

"If I had been, I would have come away with a lot more for my eight bits," Auntie went on.

"Well, you go next time. Go on. I resign," Josser shouted.

"You can't," Yappo told him. "This isn't a confab."

"He's scared of that dog," Boff jeered.

"Who wouldn't be? That definitely does it. I resign." Josser stood up, ready to walk out of the door. Mel pulled him back into his seat.

"You can't resign twice. It isn't in the rules," Yappo argued, and Auntie Bessiburger told him to shut up.

"What about his making our little Snips cry?" Mrs Baldpatch, Snips' mother, asked.

"Yes, what about that?" Mrs Gaffer joined in.

"I think you should answer the question," Gaffer said.

"I only asked her if she might spare one of her onions so we could make a decent soup," Josser protested.

"Made her cry her littles eyes out. She needed that onion for her dollies' breakfast."

"They don't eat onions. They don't eat anything," Josser yelled. "I give up. I resign." This time Mel could not hold his brother back, but Boff did, by standing in his way. Yappo was also saying repeating something three times over was against all the rules; he was thumped by Auntie Bessiburger. Gaffer suggested it was time for a break and a cup of tea, and Mrs. Gaffer declared it was high time something did get broken. They were all becoming very bad-tempered. Their bad mood was instantly changed when Boff sipped his mug of tea, grimaced, and said, "Yuk! Oh, Mrs. Gaffer, did you make this with that cabbage? It is truly awful!"

Gaffer spluttered. Mrs. Gaffer looked furious, and then everybody laughed. When Mel had produced the cabbage and said it was a 'free gift' they had been outraged. Paying eight bits for a measly few onions and carrots, a handful of dried pods, and a niggardly scoop of oatmeal had been bad enough, but they had all come through the march and knew what happened when you were desperately short of food. You paid the asking price and said 'thank you'. Even so, that limp and mouldy cabbage had been the final insult.

Gaffer said they should move on to the big order.

"I want to know what's in that purse," Mel said. "You gave Josser nine bits and he spent eight. That purse looks too fat to be holding just one bit. What's in it?" Gaffer looked uncertain.

"Go on. Tell him," Josser urged. "I won't get any rest from his nagging until you do." Gaffer picked up the purse and emptied its contents on the table.

"Them's my buttons!" Mrs. Gaffer cried in amazement. "How?"

"We did it when you were making tea, my dear."

"Behind my back! Well, you can make your own tea from now on."

There was more laughter.

"If that Mrs. Intpot finds out, she'll feed you to her dog,"

Mrs Baldpatch said.

"I'm not going back there. I've resigned," Josser told her.

"Let's get on with the order," Boff shouted. He was becoming impatient. "Start with plenty of oatmeal."

Then there was a great clamour during which item after item was added to the lengthening list. It only ended when Mel, who had not asked for a single thing, said, "This is all very well, but we have only one bit left. How are we going to pay for all this?" All eyes focused on Josser.

"Don't worry about that," he said airily. "I've worked out everything."

"I thought you'd resigned," Yappo reminded him.

"Have you got that in writing?"

"You are sure you know what you are doing?" Gaffer asked anxiously.

"Oh. Yes. But I need a couple of days at least. How long can we last out?"

All eyes turned to Aunt Bessiburger.

"I'm sure we will," she said confidently. "We always have. Ferriter's lot came back with something last night."

"Oh. A miracle at last!" Mrs. Gaffer said, and Ferriter scowled.

"What?" Mel asked.

"Half a bag of things called Jersey Royals," Aunt Bessiburger told him.

"So now we're reduced to eating a king's cast-off pullovers," Josser said.

"Don't try to explain," Mel warned. Gaffer hurriedly closed the meeting.

"I do that!" Yappo protested.

"I hope you have a plan," Mel said.

77

"No," Josser replied.

"An idea, then?"

"No. Perhaps a glimmer," Josser conceded.

"You were talking to Auntie Bessiburger. Is she involved?"

"Unfortunately." The two brothers, with Josser in the lead, were hurrying towards the rill.

"Why here?" Mel asked when they came to the water trickling downhill between the rocks and pebbles on its way to join the stream.

"Brambles."

"They're not ready for at least another month," Mel protested.

"According to Clogs, we might have to wait another two," Josser told his brother. "Here's the very man." Clogs, so called because he always wore wooden boots, was clumping down the rill towards them.

"I heard he wears those things in bed," Mel whispered.

"Ask him and find out," Josser suggested.

"While he's carrying that thing! No way," Mel said, and moved to stand behind his brother.

Clogs was carrying a very sharp curved tool known as a sickle or slasher. As he strode towards them, he swung the sickle to decapitate thistles and nettles which fell in swathes behind him. He was not given to talking, especially in sentences.

"Reckon six weeks to picking," he said. "Goodly crop. Least 60 jars. Would do, unless you were thirsty."

"And the other?" Josser asked.

"Show you the way. Can't go there without swinging this." He brandished the sickle, and Mel feared his own head might already be rolling down the rill.

They followed Clogs back up the rill to a spot where the brambles had been hacked to the ground. Clogs pointed.

"Bricks," he said. "Path."

"What's at the other end?"

"Guessing. Sloes, cherries, nuts." Clogs swung his fearsome weapon again and more brambles and nettles were toppled.

"Week to hack through," he said.

"Need you elsewhere before that," Josser told him.

"More than a week then. Keep busy," Clogs went on slashing.

"Leave you to it," Josser said.

"How do you talk to him?" Mel asked Josser as they walked on.

"Slowly. One word at a time."

"Oh." Mel had another question. "Where are we going now?"

"Auntie Bessiburger's."

"I think I may go fishing. Catch something for supper," Mel suggested because he was a little scared of Auntie Bessiburger.

"Might be a good idea. You won't get blamed if things go wrong."

"Could they?" Mel asked anxiously.

"Anything can go wrong, even when it isn't my fault." So Mel went fishing.

Auntie Bessiburger lived in an upside-down wooden box. Many years ago it had been tipped off a farm cart and rolled down to settle among the rocks, blocking a natural cavity. Auntie Bessiburger had been first to find and 'bag' it. Then she had persuaded Boff to convert the box into a neat little home with a side passage leading into the cavity which became the dwarfs' food bank. On the other side of the passage were the ovens in which Auntie Bessiburger cooked oatcakes, honey cakes, bread, and sausages, if she had anything to cook. When Josser arrived she was waiting for potato cakes to turn brown.

"Go away," she said before Josser had chance to open his mouth.

"You don't know why I'm here," Josser protested.

"Yes, I do. You're on the scrounge, as usual."

"Not for myself," Josser protested. He sniffed. "Those smell nice. Hope they don't burn."

"If they do, I'll blame you. Distracting me. Josser, what do you want?"

Josser sniffed again. "I think they are burning," he insisted.

"Then get out of my way," Auntie Bessiburger ordered. She pushed Josser to one side, opened the ovens with gloved hands and pulled out the baking trays. The potato cakes were tipped on to a sheet of greaseproof paper and separated with a large wooden spoon.

"They do look good. Ow!"

Josser had ventured to touch a potato cake and been rapped hard on the knuckles.

"I've counted them," he was warned, "so don't try sneaking one behind my back. And why are you bothering me?"

"Just for a tiny drop of the best," Josser pleaded, still rubbing the back of his hand.

Auntie Bessiburger eyed him thoughtfully.

"You aren't daft enough to ask for yourself, so I'll listen. This had better be good." So Josser explained, and after Auntie Bessiburger had listened very carefully and after she had asked a lot of questions, they went along the passage and into the food bank where Auntie Bessiburger handed her visitor a small, tightly-corked black bottle. On the way out, Josser said the potato cakes he could remember were very tasty, and the big wooden spoon was waved right under his nose with a stern warning he should stop living dangerously.

There was trout for supper, cooked, as Josser liked, with herbs and wild mushrooms.

"Did your talk with Auntie Bessiburger go well?" Mel asked.

"Yes and no," Josser replied.

"What does the 'no' mean?"

"You haven't a potato cake to go with your supper."

In the morning they walked to Aunt Sally's garden, followed by Boff, Clogs, Baldpatch, Tecky, Pipkin, Cherry, and Nerdo, who had not been invited.

"Why is he here?" Josser asked.

"He said he'd like to come along," Cherry replied.

"What's that he's got on his back?" Mel wanted to know.

"His banjo. He never goes anywhere without it."

"He did the other day."

"Because air smelled cold. The banjo is very temperamental. It's a twangy musical instrument, and if the air is cold it goes flat."

Josser interrupted their conversation. "Twangy music is definitely out," he said.

"That's all right," Cherry said, "It's broken."

Mel opened his mouth to ask why Nerdo was carrying a useless banjo, but thought that might send the conversation round in circles and decided to say nothing.

"As long as he keeps out of the way," Josser warned.

"He said he would just tag along," Cherry promised.

Before they reached the gate, Josser told most of them to stay outside the gate. Only Mel and Tecky were to accompany him.

This time the gate was wide open. There was a welcoming

81

smile on Prunella's face, and Boris, happily chewing on a bone, was chained up. Thuggydear was pedalling madly on the water wheel, making water slosh everywhere. The Aunt Sally was drenched.

"My best customer's back," Prunella cooed. She was about to greet Josser with a hug, but then she noticed something.

"No purse," she snapped. "You come, but you don't buy? We don't welcome sightseers." Josser waved the list under her long nose.

"Oh, but I'm here to buy. Just look at my list. On credit, Prunella, like it says on your board. 'Credit offered to regular and respected customers'."

"You've only been here once."

"And paid on the dot. Am I not respected? Look at the first item. 6 bags of your best oatmeal. Shall we begin there?" As Josser started to walk towards the store shed, Prunella hung back. For a moment it looked as if she were about to be very awkward and demand her money first. But, she was distracted. They were all distracted.

"Hey, man! Is that cool or is it cool?" Nerdo, who should have stayed outside with the others was still tagging along, and was standing so close to the water wheel the clanking buckets were spraying him from head to foot. Thuggydear, a big grin on his face was pedalling even faster.

"Hey, Ma, I've got me a real friend at last!" he yelled.

As Prunella hesitated, Josser tugged at her arm and bawled in her ear, for the clanking buckets were make a dreadful clatter, "And have I got deal for you. Irresistible." She was persuaded, and they went to the store shed to count sacks of oatmeal and beans.

Nerdo, still being splashed with water, spotted Boris who

was more interested in his bone.

"Hey, is that your pet? Cute," he said, and walked towards the dog. Mel closed his eyes, fearing he was about to watch Nerdo being chomped. But when Nerdo patted Boris on his head, the dog forgot his bone, licked Nerdo's hand, sat up on hind legs and begged with his forepaws.

"Oh, so cool," Nerdo said. Thuggydear, who had got off the water wheel and followed his new friend along the path, was gazing at the banjo.

"They don't play well when wet," he warned.

"That one doesn't play. It's broken," Tecky said.

"Can I have a look?" Thuggydear asked, even though he had the banjo in his hands and was already looking.

"Needs a new string or something," Tecky suggested.

"Wire," Thuggydear obviously knew about banjos.

"Got a coil in my pocket," Techy offered.

Within in minutes the banjo was restrung and Thuggydear was twanging.

"Got to tune it," he explained, giving the banjo a shake to remove the water that was sloshing around inside.

Boris, who was not a music-lover, returned to his bone. Mel, who liked twangy music almost as little as his brother, winced as the twanging increased while the peg was turned and the instrument tuned to perfection. When Thuggydear switched from tuning to playing, Nerdo was ecstatic. When Thuggydear also burst into song, his adoring mother gave up counting sacks and came out of the shed to listen. Her big feet began to move in time with the music, and Josser could only gape when Prunella started to dance. The performance ended with a loud flourish of twangs and an exaggerated bow by Thuggydear. His mother clapped.

"Takes after his father," she explained. "We met in the

circus. A very talented musician, the two-timing twister. Shall we get on with your order?"

"You were in a circus?" Mel asked when the vegetables were being carried to the gate by Tecky and Nerdo.

"Ace act," Prunella said proudly. "I was the lady contortionist."

"I wouldn't tell Josser that," Mel advised.

"Why on earth not?"

"He has the unfortunate knack of messing up long words."

Outside Boff was organising the carrying away of the vegetables. Everyone had to join in, apart from Josser and Mel who had to settle up. Thuggydear wanted to help, and was sternly warned by his mother he was not to go even one step beyond the fence.

"You know where we live?" Josser asked.

"Be daft if I didn't. You've been making homes all over the Waste. Mind the biggies don't squash you underfoot."

They never come," Josser said.

"Oh, but they do. They poke around the rill in the spring, and wade up and down the stream in the summer. You've still to meet them. Now can we get on with paying this bill?"

"On credit," Josser reminded her.

"On credit! I'll need a deposit. Credit costs." Josser handed Prunella his last one-bit coin.

"What's this?" she shrieked.

"A deposit. As agreed. No deposit too small."

"It says that on your notice," Mel pointed out. "That's what the words say."

"Those words are not in the same sentence," Prunella snapped, "and you owe me 107 bits. Round that up and allow for your deposit that's 110 bits. There's the interest. How long before you pay up?"

"Two months."

"That another twenty. You'd better have something good to offer."

"This," Josser said and produced a small, black bottle, very tightly corked. He pulled out the cork, waved the bottle under Prunella's nose and invited her to take a sip. But, before she could, Thuggydear had snatched the bottle away and poured the entire contents down his throat. Down they went with two loud glugs. Thuggydear's face went a bright red, his eyes rolled like marbles, and his smile was like the sun.

"Oh, Ma," he whispered. "Oh! Ma! Pure nectar. The fabbest tops!"

Josser offered Prunella the cork.

"Have a taste," he suggested. She licked the cork.

"How much?" she asked.

"Thirty jars?" Josser offered.

"Say forty and I might be interested," she replied.

"There are jars and there are jars," Mel, who was becoming more and more worried, warned.

"Of course," Prunella said with a beam. "How sensible. Thuggydear, fetch one of our empty oil jars and a beaker."

"Which size jar, Ma? Big or small?"

"Medium," Mel muttered.

When Thuggydear handed his mother the beaker she showed it to Josser.

"Fair is fair," she said. "Each jar must contain four full beakers. Agreed. You can take this beaker and use it as a measure."

"Thirty jars," Josser tried again.

"We agreed on forty," Prunella said sharply. There was no

more haggling,

"I hope you know what you are doing," Mel said as they were on their way home. Josser did not answer so Mel went on.

"It's three years since we've picked brambles. We picked for three whole days, and barely filled four tubs. Remember. Now you've promised forty jars, and we don't yet know how many berries we'll pick."

"You heard Clogs. 60 jars, and maybe more. Enough for both grasping Prunella and us." Mel shrugged. They walked on quite a way, before he dared speak again.

"There is one small problem," he ventured. "Clogs can't count."

Chapter 09
Brambles

Boff had come, not to discuss the new door, but to advise on a smoking chimney. Josser had lit a fire in his new fireplace and the smoke had gone everywhere but up the chimney. The smell still lingered. Boff sniffed.

"Must have been a real fog in here," he said.

"Couldn't even see him," Mel said.

"Well, there's always a little bit of good," Boff remarked. "This needs studying." As they all studied, they could hear, fortunately far away, the twangy music made by someone playing a banjo very badly.

"Nerdo," Mel said.

"And we haven't forgiven Tecky for mending that banjo," Josser added.

"You could do with a taller chimney," Boff told them. They stared at him.

"Fire ain't drawing," he explained. "Needs a good draught. The taller the chimney the stronger the draught."

"Be a giveaway," Josser pointed out. They all studied some more. That distant twanging continued, this time accompanied by singing which was completely out of tune.

"That is awful," Boff muttered.

"There is nothing wrong with my fireplace," Josser protested.

"Needs a vent," Boff told him. "Must look outside."

So they went outside and Boff poked around the roots of the

tree. The discordant twanging and singing was much louder.

"Can't he try a different tune?" Boff asked.

"He only knows one," Mel said, "or maybe there is only one and he doesn't know it. Have I said that right?"

"Got the message," Boff told him, "and, in case I make the mistake of asking for an encore, what is it called?"

"Cleaning windows," Mel said.

"Better than singing about them. Useful job," Boff told him, and turned to Josser. "Dig here," he said. "Start in your fireplace and dig a tunnel to come out here." He scratched a cross in the hard soil between two roots.

"We could make it look like a rabbit hole," Mel said.

"We don't have rabbits," Josser pointed out.

"Can you blame them?" Boff asked. "That row's enough to drive anything away."

Just as he was leaving, Boff asked how the door was getting on.

"Very nicely," Josser said, and tapped his head. "It's all worked out in here."

"H'm," Boff replied, "Must be plenty of wood under your cap."

"Sometimes I go off Boff," Josser growled as they were walking towards the rill. Before Mel could think of a suitable reply, Lib and Lus were skipping round them, both asking the same question. When was their very best friend, Penny, coming to see them? "In a few days," he told them.

"Can we come with you to the Crooked Path?" Lus begged.

"Then we can finish our hops," her sister said.

"If you tell Cherry I want to see him today, I'll think about that," Josser promised.

"Hurray!" the two little girls said and scampered off.

"Why do you want to see Cherry?" Mel asked.

"Got a job for him. Digging."

When they reached the rill, Clogs and Baldpatch were already there gazing at the ripening brambles.

"Good crop," Baldpatch predicted, "be ready for picking in a few days."

"Not for eating," Josser warned.

When Gaffer had told a packed confab about their deal with Aunt Sally's Vegetable and Fruit Garden, not everyone had been enthusiastic. Old Gab had gone as far as saying they had been robbed again just as they had 'with that mouldy cabbage'.

For once Auntie Bessiburger had been on Josser's side, pointing out that they were 'all eating again'. Limpet had been gloomy. They might be eating again, he agreed, but would they be drinking?

"Clogs said there would be enough for sixty jars," Josser had told the confab.

"Did I?" Clogs had sounded amazed. "Is sixty more than forty or less?"

Now he was looking very sheepish, and happy to leave predictions to Baldpatch, who refused to make any.

"Got a path right to the fence," Clogs mumbled.

"Then lead on," Josser told him.

As they pushed their ways towards the fence they had to contend with less brambles, but had to duck under or brush away branches.

"Orchard once," Baldpatch explained. "Fence was built right through it."

"Any fruit?" Josser asked.

"Few handfuls here and there. Couple of decent apple trees on the other side of the fence. Sloes and cherries on ours. Cherries are sour." They came to the fence. Baldpatch pointed. They could all see the gleam of green apples in the shadows.

"If only," Mel said.

"Anything else on our side?" Josser asked.

"Currants, but don't expect lots at this time of year. Everything's been neglected or gone back to wild."

"Nuts," Clogs said, "Lots of nuts."

"Can't turn them into wine," Mel said. No one was looking on the bright side.

"We'll go and talk to Limpet," Josser said.

"I wouldn't," Baldpatch advised, "And if you're being sensible, don't mention jars. He's not in the mood." Limpet lived in a green plastic tub which had once contained grass seed. It was almost hidden under a fallen tree, and the entrance was hard to find because the trunk of tree was covered with a creeping pea plant from which Limpet could pick pods. They were his favourite food, along with oatcakes spread with honey. Limpet was also in constant need of bramble wine to wash down his food, and the prospect of going without for another year had put him in a very bad mood.

"I haven't got all your jars, and I hope I never do," he told Josser bluntly.

"How many?" Josser asked, trying to be sensible and avoid the subject of bramble wine.

"You count them. I'm past caring."

The jars, and there were only twenty-seven of them, were also stored under the fallen tree, tucked away with dozens of other objects because Limpet was an avid hoarder who, true to his name, rarely gave anything away.

"Got any nails?" Josser asked.

"Not for you. Go away," Limpet replied, though he had

hundreds of nails which he kept in a locked box to prevent them from getting wet or stolen. At that moment their testy conversation was interrupted by another burst of twanging which made Limpet lose his temper completely.

"Can't anybody stop that row?" he shouted.

"If you don't like it, put your head in a bucket," Josser shouted back, leaving Limpet speechless and looking round for something to throw.

"We should go home now before your day gets worse," Mel warned.

"Must talk to Auntie Bessiburger first," Josser insisted, and walked on.

"This day is doomed," Mel predicted as he trailed after his brother.

Auntie Bessiburger was pre-occupied with removing hot honey oatcakes from her ovens. Josser and his brother were told abruptly to stand well back and keep their hands in their pockets. Aided by Mrs Mangle who also glared at them, Auntie Bessiburger deftly lifted the trays out of the ovens and tipped the contents on to a table where they would cool.

"We've counted them," Mrs Mangle warned.

"It's nice to be welcome," Mel observed.

"Oh, you are welcome as long as you keep your hands in your pockets and don't spoil things," Mrs. Mangle went on.

"What could we spoil?" Josser wanted to know.

"Your new reputation," Auntie Bessiburger told him. "Last night everyone had something for supper. Kids, mums and dads all ate something. Haven't done that for very long time. All down to you." With a flourish of her big wooden spoon right under Josser's nose, Auntie Bessiburger ended her speech with a stern warning, "So don't ruin it by going back to your old habits."

"He will," Mrs Mangle added philosophically. "They always do."

Before either Josser or Mel could think of a reply, Miss Priss, using her closed parasol as a pointer, walked in followed by a stream of toddlers.

"Look, children," she said. They looked in all directions before focussing on the table heaped with honeyed oatcakes.

"At Uncle Josser," Miss Priss told the children. "Thanks to Uncle Josser you will have bags of honeyed oatcakes to take home and share with you mummies and daddies. Now, what must we say?"

With the exception of Chatty who placed one grubby hand across his mouth, the children dutifully chorused, "Thank you, Uncle Josser."

"And to show our appreciation what are we going to do?" This time there was no response; if the toddlers had been told they had also forgotten. Miss Priss answered for them.

"We are inviting Uncle Josser to a special performance of our Kissmas play. Now, children make an orderly line so Mrs Mangle can hand out the oatcakes."

Josser and Mel stood back and watched as the children lined up and were given their oatcakes in small paper bags before being told to go straight home and not help themselves on the way. Two of the toddlers decided not to obey, but came to stare up at Josser and Mel.

"Hello, Chatty," Mel said, "Have you come to talk to me?"

"Dunno," Chatty said, and taking an oatcake out of his bag, scrunched it as he walked away.

Foggy, having looked up with his usual puzzled expression, stepped closer and stamped hard on Josser's toes, making sure he had his full attention. Then, putting one hand up to shield his mouth, he said, in a whisper loud enough to be heard on any stage, "I'm going to be a tree."

"Let's go home," Josser said, trying to walk. His foot was beginning to throb.

"I thought you wanted to talk to Auntie Bessiburger."

"I've forgotten why. I'm in shock."

"Because you're an uncle?"

"Don't remind me. Oh! Now what?" Josser groaned. Mrs. Mangle, looking grim and purposeful, was bearing down on them.

"My Tiddy says it's her turn to meet the biggie. I've already spoken to Gaffer, and he says that's your responsibility, seeing you're now the 'special friend'."

Before Josser could argue, which would have only made matters worse, Mel intervened.

"We've given that some thought," he said. "Perhaps Tiddy and one friend would like to come along with us to our next meeting. After the brambling."

"Oh!" Mrs Mangle said. "I'll hold you to that."

"I can't remember any talk," Josser said as they walked on.

"We've just had it, Uncle," Mel told him with a chuckle.

"That is not funny," Josser shouted. "You should not make fun of my adversity, especially when a so-called nephew has broken every bone in my foot!"

"Sorry," Mel said, "I promise not to laugh." But he chuckled and chortled all the way home, and even more when Josser picked up a broken branch and used it as a crutch.

Cherry was waiting. Mel warned him not to ask. Cherry listened patiently while he was advised how to dig two holes so they met in the middle. Josser showed him the fireplace and said "Dig straight down from here." Then he led him outside and with much groaning and grimacing showed him where Boff had driven a peg at a slightly upward angle between two roots.

"When you dig down from the fireplace and your spade hits this peg, you come out here and remove the peg. Understand?"

"Yes, Mr. Josser. Have you hurt your foot?"

Josser growled.

"Can't dig tomorrow," Cherry went on. "Sorry. Have to stay home and look after Lib and Lus because Ma is scrubbing tubs for the brambles. I could bring them with me, I suppose."

"Don't even think of it," Josser said. "Come when your Ma's finished scrubbing. Does she like scrubbing?"

"Don't think so. I'm never going to do scrubbing."

"Got your future all planned out? What are you going to be?"

"A forager," Cherry said promptly. "Like Ferriter. That's exciting."

"Like being kidnapped by a biggie," Josser said, and Cherry went red in the face.

"I think I should go home now," he mumbled.

Mel had to make their supper because every time his brother hobbled he groaned, loudly. As supper consisted of oatcakes and crisply fried strips of bacon, Josser finally felt well enough to ask where the bacon had come from.

"The village on the other side of the stream," Mel told him. "The pub was hosting a skittle and barbecue event in the car park. When that got really exciting, Ferriter nipped into the kitchen."

"Who went with him?" Josser asked. "No. Don't tell me. I can guess. Streaky."

"And Toga."

"Toga! Did his missus know?"

"She does now!"

"Poor Toga. Is there any of this bacon left?"

"No. You gave Cherry a bag of pods. Can we spare them?"

"Digging takes energy. He's got to eat." Mel stared at his brother.

"I think you're going soft," he said. "Turning into a proper uncle."

The next days were warm and showery. Baldpatch and Clogs, who considered themselves expert forecasters, said the showers would soon stop, the sun would shine, the brambles would turn a dark purple, becoming full of juice. Then they would be ripe for picking. On the morning when Nurse Twiggs and Pipkin, her son, came back from the bramble bushes with their hands stained a deep dark purple everyone knew the picking had begun. They all joined in, filling baskets with the precious berries and taking them to Auntie Bessiburger's where the fruit was rinsed and placed in deep buckets of water, so the leaves and bad berries would rise to the top and be skimmed off.

Limpet, who reckoned they would have to fill sixty buckets twice over, watched anxiously and fretted. He was not the only one to worry. Ferriter, who had promised Auntie Bessiburger faithfully he would return with enough sugar and yeast, had not come back. His fellow foragers, Streaky and Toga were also missing, and a distraught Mrs. Toga was weeping into her emptied berry basket. Auntie Bessiburger assured her everything would turn out right, and if it didn't 'that Ferriter was a dead dog'.

As Josser and Mel were staggering home, weary after a day picking in the hot sun, they were met by an anxious Mrs. Bobble who wanted to know where her son was.

"He should be digging," Josser said. "He should have finished."

But when they went to look, followed by Lib and Lus, they saw only a rather dented spade standing by a hole which was clearly not finished.

"Look what he's done to my spade!" Josser shouted

"At least, he hasn't fallen down here," Mel said as he looked into the hole.

"Maybe he's fallen right through, and landed in Australia. He'll be eaten by a kangaroo," Josser yelled, and Lib and Lus started to wail.

"You've done it again," Mel told him, before escorting Mrs. Bobble and her daughter's home.

"Now for supper," Josser said.

"Oatcakes," Mel told him.

"Prunella should have kept chickens. Then we could have had scrambled eggs on oatcakes. For a change," Josser said, sounding wistful.

"You don't like scrambled eggs."

"I do like a change." Before they could get this argument going, Boff was with them.

"If you had a door I would have knocked on it," he said, "Just come to tell you Toga is back."

"Is his missus happy?"

"She will be when she's made him miserable. Streaky is also back with his pockets full of sugar."

"What about Cherry?" Josser asked.

"Then you knew he'd gone with them!"

"Worked it out. Go on."

"Ferriter's carrying him back.

"Is he hurt? Is he dead?" Mel asked in great alarm.

Boff grinned.

"Oh! He'll live, but he won't be happy. He's dead drunk."

Chapter 10
The Rules of Hops.

The picking must go on. The berries had to be stripped from their clinging branches until there were no more to pick. There was a lot of talk during the picking, but Gaffer had been very firm. Dealing with Cherry would have to wait. Mrs Bobble had to leave her son, pale, tearful and, at times, very sick, lying on his bed, and entirely at the mercy of his little sisters.

"I can't imagine a worse punishment," she told Mrs. Mangle. "Has he told you what happened?"

"He has shouted out that he did it, but then he's sick and can't say any more."

"I heard Ferriter took him into that pub, the 'Bap and Bottle'," whispered Nurse Twiggs. "A grown man like that leading a sweet little boy to drink. He should be punished."

"Oh, he will be," Mrs. Bobble promised her.

At Aunt Bessiburger's the tubs were being filled with a solution of hot water and sugar. The bramble berries, carefully measured and packed in straining bags, were placed in the solution which was heated until it began to bubble. Then the tubs were removed from the hot slabs and left to stand while the liquid in them fermented. That would take days during which yeast and other ingredients would be added, according to the secret recipe known only to a very few.

Known only to Auntie Bessiburger, Ferriter was hiding in her living room while the winemaking continued. He was dozing because he hadn't slept for twenty-four hours. The other villain,

Streaky, was pretending to help a very morose Limpet wash his collection of forty jars and bottles, while listening to an endless complaint that they were never going to pick enough brambles. Streaky, who had already been warned by Mrs. Baldpatch that this time 'he was really in for it', had a grumble of his own. No one was blaming Toga who had been smacked and then forgiven by his wife; he was being let off simply because he was too easily led. Streaky kept muttering that was 'unfair'.

By the middle of the third afternoon there were no berries left to pick. Clogs and Baldpatch went to look for sloes and nuts. The last berries were put in washing buckets. The line of cooling tubs was a little longer, and Ferriter felt brave enough to sneak off and explain to Gaffer why Cherry had to be carried home drunk. Josser and Mel had been invited to join the interrogation; Mrs. Gaffer invited herself.

"He didn't get drunk," Ferriter explained. "He fell in one of those fizzy drinks with a cherry on a stick and a funny name."

"Cocktail," Mel said.

"That right," Ferriter agreed.

"Can we start at the very beginning?" Gaffer asked.

"Yes. Digging a hole in my fireplace," Josser pointed out.

"That's where he was," Ferriter admitted, "And that was a rotten spade you gave him. Couldn't dig a hole in butter."

"Stick with the story," Gaffer warned.

"Yes. Well, Auntie Bessiburger wanted brandy and sugar. The only place we could get them was the 'Bap and Bottle'. Sugar is easy. They keep it in a big bag under the counter in the morning coffee room. You can sneak in, climb up on to the shelf and fill your pockets."

"Like Streaky and Toga?" Mrs. Gaffer asked.

"That's right, only Toga came away with a pocketful of

coffee as well. His missus likes coffee."

"Didn't save him," Josser pointed out.

"Get on with it," Gaffer snapped, feeling he was about to get another headache.

"Brandy is difficult," Ferriter explained. "They keep it in a locked glass cabinet labelled 'Spits'."

"Spirits," Mel corrected him.

"Whatever. I wasn't there for no reading lesson," Ferriter said, sounding cross. "You can't get in because it's locked, unless you're little and can wriggle through a hole in the top and undo the catches which keep the wooden back in place."

"Can you follow that?" Gaffer asked Mel.

"I think so," Mel replied. "They took Cherry along because he was thin enough to get through a hole."

"When he should have been digging one," Josser added.

"Not with that spade," Ferriter said. "Downright cruel to give a kid a spade that wouldn't dig."

"At least it wouldn't get him drunk," Josser argued.

"Yes," Mrs. Gaffer said, "How did Cherry get drunk?"

"I've told you. He wriggled through the hole and fell into a glass. It was full."

"And then?" Gaffer prompted.

"He got out of the glass, and managed to open a couple of the catches. I don't know how. He was a hero! We got the backboard open, helped him out and sat him on the counter to come to his senses. Got the brandy, tidied the cabinet, put the board back. Leave no traces. That's the rule and we kept to it, but then Cherry didn't come to his senses. Did he? He was dancing all over the counter, waving his arms about, and singing. It was lucky no one heard. Then he flopped. We got him outside and I told the others to come home."

"Brought him home on your own," Gaffer murmured.

"With the brandy. Daren't come back without it," Ferriter told them.

Gaffer told the forager to go home and get some sleep. Pipkin arrived and handed Gaffer a message. He read it and shook his head.

"Bad news for you, Josser," he said. "Aunt Bessiburger reckons she'll make just enough wine to fill fifty jars. At a pinch. She won't tell anyone else yet. And, before I forget, you are meeting the biggie tomorrow. Not a word about this must reach her."

"Don't see how we can stop that," Josser grumbled on the way home.

"Just tell Cherry's sisters not to talk about their brother," Mel advised.

"You tell them. They're girls. They're just like their mum. Tell her not to talk about something and she'll tell everyone."

"You are in a bad mood," Mel said.

Boff arrived with the refurbished spade. It looked clean and shiny. He banged it into the hard-baked earth. Sparks flew, but the ground was hardly chipped.

"Cherry can't do much with this," he warned.

"He's started. He's been paid. He'll finish," Josser said.

"You are hard," Boff told him, and then grinned. "But then you'll need to be, seeing you've given away all our bramble wine."

"Everybody knows!" Josser was shocked.

"Limpet knows. He's making sure they all do."

The Crooked Path seemed to be full of girls playing their own versions of hops or just watching. Snips was missing because she was making certain her dollies ate up all their

100

breakfast, and, much to Josser's relief, so were Lib and Lus.

"I thought we decided there would only be four," Mel said, as he and his brother made their way down to the bridge where they planned to wait on their side of the gate. But PALS, or Penny, as she was called by all the girls, had arrived.

"I think we should talk," she said.

"Oh dear!" Mel said. "I think she knows."

"Well, Poges Minor is our village," Penny said sternly. They stared at her in amazement,

"Poggis belongs to you?" Josser asked

"We live in the big house just beyond. There was a time when everyone in the village worked for the lord living in the big house, and it is 'Po Jes' and not 'Poggis' which sounds like the name for a cat."

"Moggies," Mel said, "And that means more than one cat."

"You are both as bad as one another," Pals declared.

"Have you come to lecture us?" Josser asked.

"You deserve a lecture after what you did in our pub. And I'm here to meet my friends."

Two smiling girls were already walking towards them.

"Tiddy and Bibba," Mel said. "Tiddy wants to teach you her version of hops. She's the one with the stick of chalk."

"All right," Penny agreed.

"You can mark out your shapes," Mel told the girls and they went away to find the smoothest stretch of path.

"They're not the same," Penny said. "Tiddy is like Lib or Lus. Bibba isn't. She's coloured."

"Bibba isn't different," Josser said. "Just her skin. Inside she's just the same as Tiddy, or Lib, or Lus. They're all persons."

"Oh!" Penny sounded hurt. "Have I said something wrong?"

"No. Daft. Now go and play. We can finish our conversation

101

later," Josser told her.

"And let them win. They're only little," Mel added.

"She thinks we did it," Josser sounded worried.

"If we try to tell her it wasn't us, she'll keep on asking questions and we'll end up telling her all about Ferriter," Mel pointed out.

"Let's pretend we know absolutely nothing," Josser suggested.

Then they watched the hops and hoped. After a while only one game of hops was being played. While all the others girls watched intently. Penny was taking on Tiddy and Bibba.

"Do you understand this game?" Josser asked his brother.

"No," Mel told him. "There are rules, but the most important rule is that you can change them. Does that make sense to you?"

They heard clapping and some cheers. Little girls were jumping up and down in excitement.

"Final round," Mel said. "They will be using Lib's running rule. Tiddy to run and jump first."

There was a long and tense silence which ended with dismayed cries of "Oh! Tiddy!"

"In case you didn't understand that, Tiddy just landed with a toe outside a square," Mel said.

Then it was Bibba's turn. She ran and jumped faultlessly, her little feet landing in the middle of every shape. There were shrieks and hugs which were shared with Lib and Lus who had just arrived.

"Cherry must be feeling better," Mel said, but not even Josser was listening. Like all the girls he was watching the biggie jumping from shape to shape and taking her time. When she made ready for her very last jump, the tension for some girls was so high they had to close their eyes. Then Penny jumped. There

102

was a silence and then a long 'Ooh!' followed by a gasp and a cheer. "Bibba's won!" The clapping and cheering became frantic. Everyone was jumping up and down. In the middle of all the commotion, Penny picked up Lus who was whispering eagerly in her ear.

"I think you should prepare for the worst," Mel warned his brother.

The wild applause stopped when Penny put down Lus and marched towards the two brothers. The girls became an entranced audience when the biggie, stopping a few paces short, pointed an accusing finger at Josser and Mel, and said very loudly, "I know what you did. It was disgraceful!" She put her hands on her hips and stamped her foot so hard Josser and Mel clung to each other and looked away in mock terror.

"Lib has told me everything. You made poor Cherry dig a hole. Then you pretended he had reached Australia, but took him off to the pub to celebrate. You got him drunk, made him dance all over the counter, and left him to find his own way home. Disgusting!" Again she stamped her foot.

Josser look at his brother.

"Did we do all that?" he asked.

"Can't remember," Mel replied. "Must have been too drunk." They started laughing so much they fell over and rolled around. Penny was speechless. Josser picked himself.

"I'm sorry," he said, but he did not sound at all apologetic. "Did I hear you say 'Lib'?"

"You saw us. She was whispering in my ear," Penny said.

Mel who was also back on his feet said, "That wasn't Lib. That was Lus."

"Who is such a good story teller, she'll write novels when she grows up," Josser added. Penny whirled around to look for the sisters. All the children were gone.

"You see," Josser said quietly. "We are all the same."

"And we didn't take Cherry to the pub," Mel.

Penny stared down at them. She looked both angry and upset, but she said nothing.

"Cherry went because Ferriter asked him," Mel explained very quietly.

"He went because he wanted to help."

"To steal sugar," Penny managed to say.

"Forage," Josser insisted.

"That's just another word for stealing," Penny argued.

"We have rules," Mel told her. "We never take from ourselves, and we only take what we need."

"Don't forget the 'if's'," Josser added. "If it ain't nailed down, if no one's looking after it, and if it's useful and can be carried, it can be foraged." Penny rallied. She put her hands on her hips and glared down at them.

"That is absolutely disgraceful," she declared. "That means if you came across a baby sleeping in its pram, while it's mummy was in the house washing dishes, you would grab it and run away."

"Steal a baby biggie!" Josser yelled. "We aren't that daft. Baby biggies ain't useful. They sleep when they should be awake. They guzzle, and when everyone wants to sleep they bawl for hours." Both brothers were eager to enjoy a really good argument, but Penny insisted on knowing why they needed all that sugar.

"To make bramble wine," Josser said.

"So we could eat," Mel explained, but then he had to explain everything because Penny pointed out people don't eat wine. She kept on asking very serious questions, even though she did laugh when she heard Cherry had fallen into a cocktail. But she still had another question, because she wanted to win the argument.

"Why did they steal, sorry, forage coffee?"

"Toga loves coffee," Josser said.

"Bibba's dad," Mel explained. "No one else really likes coffee."

"Ah! He must be different," Penny said firmly. She was turning the argument full circle; Josser was having none of that.

"But we are still the same," Josser said.

"But I've won. Now it's time for me to go home. When can I come again?"

"Maybe Kissmas," Josser said.

"He means Christmas. Toddlers call it Kissmas and it's their big celebration," Mel added.

"Can't come then," Penny said. "Papa makes us go to Scotland where he owns a distillery."

"MacSnuffles come from Scotland," Josser told her. "Now, he is different. Comes from a place called Lancashire."

"He means Lanarkshire, but he is right about MacSnuffles. He is definitely different though he does try to be the same. What a pity you can't meet him," Mel added.

"I could come after Christmas," Penny offered.

"In time for Josser's special occasion," Mel suggested.

"What's that?"

"The grand opening of his new door."

"You must give me an invitation. You know where I live."

They had reached the gate. Penny climbed over it while they climbed up it until their heads were on a level with hers. Penny stared at them.

"I suppose you are the same," she admitted. Then she grimaced and screwed up her nose. "But you don't look the same." She pointed at Mel. "You are a nice clean sunburn colour." Her finger moved to point and wag at Josser. "But you are a total scruff. Bye."

When the brothers got home, Cherry and Pipkin were sitting on the ground where the new door would go, if it was ever finished. The refurbished spade was lying by Cherry and it looked as battered as it had before Boff took it away. Pipkin, who was leaning on a pick, saw them first.

"Hello," he said, "We got through, but we didn't get through, if you see what I mean. And Cherry's been sick. Just a little bit."

Josser picked up the spade, went to the hole in his fireplace and poked the spade down. They heard a dull sound as if the spade was hitting something soft. Josser tried again and they heard a clank as if the spade was hitting metal.

"That's not Boff's peg," Mel said.

Just then they heard Gaffer's voice.

"Hello, I thought you were ill," they heard him say.

"He is, Mr. Gaffer, and he's been sick," Pipkin replied.

"Then be a good fellow and take him home. He can always come back tomorrow." A moment or two later Gaffer was standing by the brothers and looking down at the hole.

"I won't ask why, but I think that spade needs throwing away," he paused to clear his throat, "Yes, definitely. I came to tell you the good news, but there isn't any. Auntie Bessiburger thinks she can fill fifty-three bottles or jars with bramble wine. Is thirteen an unlucky number? Limpet thinks it is, because he's demanding a confab."

Chapter 11
Kissmas

Limpet did not get his confab, and went into a long sulk. He did not get his way because Auntie Bessiburger told everyone they should be grateful to Josser; every household had food to put on the table. She also pointed out that, while Cherry was a classic example of what happened if the young were allowed too much of the demon drink, Josser had not been directly involved. For once he found himself on the right side of the ladies, even though Mrs. Mangle went around muttering, "It will never last."

"Pull the peg out," Boff advised when he came to see what had gone wrong down the hole. He was also very rude about the spade, and told Josser he was irresponsible for allowing Cherry to use it. Then they tried to pull the peg free from the outside and failed utterly.

"It's jammed," Boff said.

Josser, who always hated being told the obvious, shouted back at him.

"What flavour is it, then? Strawberry or raspberry?" That nearly started a fight, but Mrs. Mangle who happened to be passing suggested they twisted before trying to pull, and demonstrated with one powerful twist of her hands. She followed that with a gentle pull which brought the peg out of the hole.

"I won't expect any of you gentleman to say 'Thank you'," she declared as she stalked away. Nobody was listening for all eyes were on the object Boff was dragging out of the hole.

"It's some kind of glove," Mel said, as he scraped away the

dirt.

"A riding glove," Boff decided. "A very old one, called a gauntlet, can be worth a few bits."

"Where?" Josser asked.

"In a junk shop, I suppose."

"I can't see any junk shops round here."

"Plenty back where the Navs live," Boff remarked.

"Well, when I've a couple of years to spare, I'll pop back," Josser snapped.

"What shall I do with this glove?" Mel asked.

"Oh, dump it in the store room. Cherry can clean it up when he's better."

"You are in a snappy mood," Mel said, after Boff had departed carrying the unfortunate spade and warning it would never be the same again.

"Work it out," Josser said. "We have enough food to last for couple of months, but after that, nothing in our food bank, and nothing we can sell. Can't turn stones into bramble wine. It's going to be a long and thin winter, and even if we all join Ferriter and go foraging, where can we go? Poggis hasn't got a shop. He doesn't come back from that garden centre with much."

"Plenty of time for worrying. Look on the bright side."

"Is there one?"

"Kissmas. Remember you're going to be a special guest."

"Oh, joy!" Josser said, but he refused to be cheered up.

The promised jars and bottles of bramble wine were delivered, and Prunella counted every one, refusing to sign a receipt before both she and Thuggydear had tasted for themselves. Only then was she amicable.

"Been nice doing business with you," she told Josser. "We must do this again next year, if you're still on the Waste."

"Why shouldn't we be?" he asked.

"Well, you have been moving on. How many years is it now? Ten? Twenty? Three years back you were sharing that filthy tunnel with the Navs. Took you two more years to get here, and we're only seven miles away."

"Biggie miles," Josser pointed out.

"Of course. Well, maybe you will settle here and make wine. I could sell all you make. At a fair price, of course."

"Of course," Josser echoed.

"And it's so nice for Thuggydear to have a friend of his own age. What is he called? Nerdo? Isn't that a Nav name?"

Josser wished she would just stop talking, but Prunella had something more to say.

"Perhaps you'll decide to move on. You've never got on with your neighbours, have you? And the Bats have been in those mines for ever such a long time. Then there's the biggies, traipsing along the stream and up and down the rill."

"They miss you," Josser pointed out.

"Don't come through the fence, do they? When they're clumping up and down the rill, we go on holiday. Only for a few days every spring."

When Josser reported this conversation Gaffer sighed.

"I suppose we must do business with that wretched witch," he said.

"Is she a witch?" Josser asked.

"She magicked our wine out of you for a pittance," Mrs Gaffer snapped. "Poor old Limpet is heartbroken."

"You don't like Limpet," Josser protested.

"Doesn't mean I shouldn't feel sorry for him when I want to."

"Perhaps a nice cup of tea will calm all of us down, my dear,"

Gaffer suggested.

"Of course," Mrs Gaffer stomped off to her kitchen.

"I thinks she likes me less than Limpet," Josser said. Gaffer ignored the remark.

"You could ask your biggie," he suggested.

"My biggie!" Josser exclaimed.

"You were elected her special friend." Before Josser could think of a suitable reply Mrs. Gaffer returned with two mugs of tea which she banged down the table.

"No biscuits," she snapped, and disappeared into her kitchen again.

"Thank you, my dear," Gaffer called after her, but the only reply was a door slam.

"What about that boy, Thuggydear?" he asked.

"Let him meet Nerdo," Josser suggested. "One way of finding out what tricks his mother is planning."

"H'm," Gaffer pondered. "You do know Miss Priss has asked Nerdo to play his banjo at the Kissmas celebrations?"

"I fear the worst," Josser said.

Most dwarfs would have liked their vegetables and fruit to grow in rows like those in Aunt Sally's Vegetable and Fruit Garden. It was very orderly with a path right down the middle. Tecky had told everyone about the wondrous waterwheel, and the weeded rows of carrots, onions, peas and beans. All was very different from their gardens which were mixed up muddles of mostly pods and beans. They had to be that way because anything as neat and tidy as Prunella's garden hidden behind high hedges would have been a 'giveaway' to nosy biggies.

So they were all busy picking the last of their pods and beans and storing them away before winter came, and it was a blessing that all of the toddlers and also Lib and Lus were busy rehearsing their Kissmas play. Even the toddlers knew about Aunt Sally's Vegetable and Fruit Garden because Thuggydear had told Nerdo how he used to throw conkers at that terrifying scarecrow, Aunt Sally. Nerdo could not resist telling the toddlers.

"I can't throw a conker. Impossible," Foggy said.

"You are a conker," Lus told him.

"Is that why I'm going to be a tree?" Foggy asked.

Before Lus could think up an answer, Miss Priss told them to go home and learn their lines.

"What's your line?" Lib asked Chatty.

"Dunno," he said.

"You know it already. Aren't you clever?" Lib said.

As they were going home, they heard Miss Priss telling Nerdo he had to play nice and gentle music for the play. 'Cleaning windows' was definitely out.

Josser had his own jobs to do. Tecky had found a length of car radiator hose which fitted into the hole in the fireplace and poked out between the roots. They had put it into place, packed gravel and sand around it to make it firm and were about to light a fire. Then they would see if the smoke rushed up the chimney as Boff had promised. Mel decided he did not want to watch and went fishing, but Pipkin and Cherry came just to see the fun. They stood well back. At first the fire flickered as flames ate into the paper, then the dried twigs caught fire and, very soon after, the chunks of wood were ablaze. Both smoke and sparks were going up the chimney.

Cherry and Pipkin came closer to admire.

"If I wasn't going to be a forager," Cherry said, "I would like to be like Tecky. He is useful."

"Who says you're going to be a forager?" Josser asked. Cherry went red.

"Well, Ferriter says I'm a natural," he mumbled.

"You're a natural at falling down, falling out of, and falling into. Being a forager requires being a natural at coming back with things people need. You have a long way to go."

"Hello everybody," Mel was back with two small fish. "Did I hear Cherry was going somewhere?"

"Back home to do some thinking. Right now," Josser said and the two boys walked away. While Josser was making sure they had gone, Mel was giving Tecky, who said he must go to get on with the stage, one of his catch because he deserved a reward for making something in Josser's house work properly.

Rehearsing was wearing Miss Priss out. That is what she told Mrs. Gaffer. She was promptly offered a cup of comforting tea, over which she admitted that teaching Nerdo to twang at the right moment was getting her down. Thanks to Lib and Lus, who had taken over everything else with enthusiasm, Miss Priss had been left with no more than the musical accompaniment which she herself would provide by tinkling on her xylophone. All Nerdo was expected to do was twang loudly on his banjo whenever the cast required a signal to do something. He was, she admitted to a sympathetic Mrs Gaffer, a willing but wayward pupil.

"He is always asking if he can play and sing 'Cleaning Windows'," she moaned.

"I hope he doesn't know the words," Mrs. Gaffer said. "He's like MacSnuffles. You can't trust amateur musicians."

Thanks to Lib and Lus, the 'Trees' — Foggy was one — had trunks made out of the cardboard cylinder found in biggie toilet rolls. These were painted grey and green because even toddlers knew tree trunks were that colour and not the bright brown favoured by biggie children. The 'Fairies' had wands made from plastic flower stakes sprayed with silver paint and capped with a golden foil star. The 'Biggies' all wore baggy trousers to hide their stilts, all made by Boff, while the 'Peskies' wore frightening masks made by cutting up biggie egg boxes and painting them black with yellow circles where the eyes went. Ferriter told everyone he was giving up foraging because he was worn out with visiting the garden centre he had just discovered; it was miles from anywhere.

Lib and Lus made sure the cast were present for all rehearsals, and knew all their lines. Snips had to be coaxed by allowing her to bring her dollies, and arrange them on a reserved seat made from two foil containers. This special seat was placed in the front row of the audience. Tecky had erected the stage in the Dell, and while the toddlers were rehearsing, some of the older children were putting up decorations.

The mums approved of all this activity which kept their children busy. Even Mrs. Mangle went as far as to say the days leading up to Kissmas had been the quietest she had ever known. She did however become very annoyed when she discovered Tiddy had borrowed her best sheets to use as stage curtains.

While Miss Priss went on believing she was producing the toddlers' play, Gaffer was busy organising the evening's programme, which meant he did exactly what he was told by Mrs. Gaffer. The entertainment would begin with a Presentation. That would be followed by an In Memoriam spoken by Slikky who would be both eloquent and dignified. Auntie Bessiburger would then make a very Special Announcement about sloe gin, before Angus MacSnuffles tottered on stage to recite a poem by someone called Robbie Burns. Mrs Gaffer longed to remove his item from the programme, but had not dared because it was so popular.

The toddlers' play rounded off the evening's entertainment.

Mrs. Gaffer had once tried putting it first, but, as soon as the toddlers' part was over, they had become noisy and restless, saying loudly they 'wanted to go'. Josser had suggested putting it last because then they would wait in silence. He had been right. For once.

Apart from Snip's dollies, who had their own special seat, and Josser who had a chair borrowed from Mrs. Gaffer's parlour, the audience sat as they usually did, with the men using their second-best hats and the ladies bringing cushions. Gaffer bid everyone welcome to their very first Kissmas in the Low Wood, and hoped there would be many more. He then introduced Josser as 'their special guest for the evening'. Josser took a bow and was loudly booed by Limpet.

Much to his surprise and embarrassment, Cherry was called on to the stage to receive an embroidered badge bearing a single capital letter 'F' because he had become a forager. Everyone applauded loudly. Even Streaky clapped though he was heard complaining that he had been a forager for years but 'no one had given him as much as a thank you'.

Slikky Bo reminded his audience of their hard and harrowing time when crossing the desert with only a cup of water each day, and their monotonous diet of dried insects known as 'locust scrunchies'. The usual trouble makers, sitting at the back, pretended to fall asleep and snore.

Auntie Bessiburger woke them up by showing the audience a jar labelled 'Sloe Gin' and saying there would be a 'nip' for every grown up when the show was over. Streaky shouted 'Can we go home now?" and was thumped by Mrs. Mangle. Yappo had to tell everyone to 'settle down' because Angus was waiting to entertain them as he had done every Kissmas since he had joined the march.

As he had recited the same poem every year, his performance came as no surprise. Most of the audience knew his recitation by heart, and, as he performed, their lips could be seen mouthing the words; but they enjoyed it just same. As Mel said, 'MacSnuffles' acting was so bad you could not help enjoying it.'

Angus strutted to the front of the stage, glared at his audience, and banged three times on the boards with his crooked walking stick. Then he waved it dramatically before announcing, "A Poem by the Greatest Poet this side of the Milky Way, Robbie Burns"

"Is he on fire?" Streaky shouted.

"Put him out," Clogs added. Angus pointed his walking stick at them.

"You, sirs, are a couple of uncouth, bandy-legged, flop-eared, goggly-eyed Sassenachs. You have no more appreciation of the fine arts than a poor wee timorous slug." The audience cheered. Yappo banged for silence. Josser who usually joined in the banter, remembered, only just in time, he was the honoured guest and forbidden, by Mel, from hurling insults at the actors.

"Angus Macsnuffles will now recite," Yappo declared. Angus cleared his throat, a noisy act in which half the audience joined.

"O, my love has got a big red nose
Which often runs in June.
It also runs on chilly nights
When we sit beneath the moon.'"

There were more verses which the audience knew so well they were whispering the words to themselves or stuffing handkerchiefs into their mouths to stop laughing. When Angus bowed and walked off, they all stood and cheered. Josser wished he could join them.

No one ever knew the plot, if there ever was one, of the toddlers' play. The performance began with a single twang of Nerdo's banjo. To a gentle tinkling by Miss Priss on her xylophone, the curtains were drawn back to reveal a tableau of Fairies, Biggies, Peskies, and Trees.

"Aw!" went all the mums. "Aren't they sweet?"

The Fairies waved their wands. The Biggies clumped about on stilts, and the Peskies hissed at each other through their masks. The Trees wagged their branches so vigorously several fell off. Everything was going as it should. Then the Trees shuffled to the front of the stage. Miss Priss raised one finger. Nerdo, who was paying attention, twanged once. That was the signal for the Trees to turn left and march off the stage. However, Chatty, who was the Tree on the very left, turned right. Foggy, who was the next Tree in the line, bumped into him and staggered backwards knocking the third Tree right off the stage. Shedding all his branches at once, the third Tree rolled into the front row of the audience, knocking Snip's dollies all over the place. They clattered on to the ground like noisy skittles.

"My dollies," Snips screamed. She threw away her wand, barged through the Biggies, trod on a Peskie, kicked the fourth Tree off the stage, gathered up her fallen dollies, and headed for home. The other Fairies threw away their wands, wailed 'mummy' and rushed headlong into the audience seeking consolation. Miss Priss, totally stricken and in tears, slumped across her silent xylophone while Nerdo, completely lost in a world of his own, changed from twanging dutifully to strumming his version of 'Cleaning Windows' hitting all the right notes though not necessarily in the right order.

And Josser? He could sit still no longer. He was on his feet, clapping loudly and shouting, "More! Encore! Brill! The best ever shindig! Encore!"

Chapter 12
The Special Occasion

The five dwarfs were talking very quietly, as though they were afraid of being overheard. And so they should, because they were talking about the night before, and their part in the chaotic ending to the toddlers' Kissmas play. Two, Baldpatch and Clogs had dared to clap and cheer, neither had been forgiven by Mrs Baldpatch.

"What happened to you this morning?" Clogs asked.

"I was told to get my own breakfast and not to speak," Baldpatch admitted, "And you're not to come round for at least a month."

"Streaky's in worse bother," Mel told them. "Auntie Bessiburger hit him because he dropped the jar. Or was it the other way round? She hit Streaky, making him drop the jar?

"I suppose we can all blame it on Josser," Clogs suggested.

"Oh, please do," Josser insisted. "After all I wasn't the one who turned right when I should have turned left."

"Chatty did that, but he's a toddler," Mel pointed out. "Toddlers can't be blamed for anything."

"And he didn't shout 'Brill! Encore! Best ever shindig!' That's what made my missus mad," Baldpatch pointed out.

Tecky, who was even less talkative than usual, had not said a word. He was leading them to where the rill ran from under the Great Roar and into the shade of the trees. On their way they had to pass Limpet who was sitting on the doorstep of his house. Above his head was a placard reading 'Give us back our bramble wine'. When Limpet saw Josser approaching, he stood up and shouted, "Got less friends now, Josser?".

He shook his fist, and went back inside his house, slamming the door after him.

"You've lost another friend," Mel said.

"Have I got any left?" Josser asked.

"Unlikely," Mel told him, "Though Auntie Bessiburger stuck up for you. Said no one should bother about you, because you couldn't help behaving the way you did. Despite all your years you were still a big kid."

Tecky stopped and sighed. He shook his head, took off his hat, and rubbed his nose.

"Can't do it," he said. They stared at him in amazement.

"Have I lost you as a friend?" Josser asked.

"Well, you asked me to do something, and now I'm telling you I can't, even though I could because it's simple, but I don't think I should. Oh dear! I don't think you understand."

"Agreed," Josser said.

"He's mixed up," Mel said, "Perhaps he should start at the beginning, if he knows where that is."

"I fell over this," Tecky explained and showed them a wooden strip with a jagged end. On it was some fading writing none of them could read.

"I think is part of a plant label," Mel said, "A biggie plant label."

"I know what it is," Tecky said crossly, "Because I fell over it and it hurt. The point is it isn't the only one. I found more than a dozen just where the rill runs into the trees."

They walked the rest of the way in silence.

"Can't go messing with these," Tecky told them when they reached the spot where the rill became several trickles between stones surrounded by mud in which grew plants, some of them partly submerged in the shallow water. They could all see plant labels sticking up by the clumps with limp dark green leaves.

"You can't," Josser agreed. "Nobody can. Biggies have marked these."

"Perhaps Prunella knows something about these. Do not disturb," Mel suggested.

"And now I've told you?" Tecky asked.

"We'll check to see if there are any more labels sticking around. You go home and say nothing," Josser told him. Mel put his arm round Tecky's shoulder.

"And don't worry," he said, "You're still a friend."

"Is that a good thing?" Tecky sounded doubtful. "I mean you never know who he's going to upset next, do you?"

"Don't worry," Mel repeated. "Think of it this way. You're only a friend. I'm his brother."

"We all feel sorry for you," Clogs said to Mel.

They watched Tecky trudge downhill.

"You three can look for more labels," Josser said. "I'm going to have a word with Limpet."

"Why?" Mel asked.

"I want to borrow some nails. I am just a big kid and no one should bother about me. So I am going to get on with my door."

"How can you borrow nails?" Baldpatch asked.

They found no more plant labels. Clogs went down as far as the bramble bushes to make sure, but none of them dared mention the fact that if there had been plants with labels by the brambles they would have been trodden underfoot during the picking. They decided to go home.

Limpet was sitting on his doorstep again, but this time he was crying.

"Josser was very rude to me," he explained.

"Josser is rude to everyone," Mel reminded him, and Limpet sniffed.

"Being rude to everyone is not the same as being very rude to an old friend who was on the march with him," he protested. "Did I not share the last of my locust scrunchies with him when we were crossing the desert? There was no reason for him to be so rude." Then Limpet started to cry again and they stared at him.

"He only wanted to borrow some nails," Clogs pointed out.

"I gave him some nails," Limpet said. "That's when he became really rude because they weren't shiny. What's the point of being shiny? You only bang nails into wood. How can you see the rust?"

"You gave him rusty nails." Mel shook his head. "For his door! Now he'll be in a bad mood with everyone. I think I'll go fishing."

"Can I join you?" Baldpatch asked. "Be more peaceful than going home."

When Mel finally got home, without any fish, the unfinished door was hidden under their collapsed tent.

"Nobody sees it," Josser told him, "Not until the day I open it for the first time."

"You upset Limpet," Mel said.

"I only asked for a handful of his best nails. What about those labels?"

"Didn't spot any more. I think we'd better talk to Gaffer." Josser sighed.

"Will I ever be allowed to finish my door?" he asked. "Yes, we have to talk to Gaffer, and I know what he's going to say. Talk to the biggie."

"Why don't you have a word with your biggie friend?" Gaffer suggested. "You are inviting her to your special occasion."

"She invited herself," Josser pointed out. Gaffer ignored his interruption.

"Cherry can take the invitation," he went on. "He has been there so he must know his way around. Be his first mission as a forager. You must go as well, of course. Both of you."

"What a good idea," Mel said, with no enthusiasm whatsoever.

"Sorry, but I can't stop to make you tea," Mrs Gaffer said. "I'm on my way to Mrs. Toga's coffee morning. Do you like my new hat, dear?" She had bustled into the room to stand in front of their cracked mirror and put on a hat which seemed to be a mix of feathers and flowers.

"Of course I do, dear," Gaffer said, though he wasn't even looking. "You go ahead. I'll see our visitors out."

"Looked like a bird's nest," Josser said. "Coffee morning! What is a coffee morning? What's wrong with tea?"

"It's the latest fashion," Mel explained, "They've all discovered coffee, and they drive Ferriter mad. He says finding coffee is worse than finding jelly babies."

Just then Lib and Lus appeared, deliberately standing in their way and pulling faces.

"We hate you," Lus shouted.

"You ruined our play. We both hate you," Lib added.

Before running away, they both pulled even more hideous faces.

"There's gratitude for you," Mel said. "When I last saw them at the Kissmas they were shrieking with laughter and clinging on to each other so they wouldn't fall over."

"Ferriter's here," Mel warned. Josser hurriedly covered his door.

"It's all right," Ferriter said, "I won't look. When will it be finished?"

"Next Kissmas, if I get any more interruptions. Why are you here?"

"To take you beyond Poggis."

"Po jess," Mel corrected him.

"Poggis sounds fine to me. Can't leave this mission to Cherry," Ferriter told them. "Got to think of the dogs."

"Dogs! What dogs!"

"Biggies' dogs. We have to go through the village, and where there's biggies there are always dogs being taken walkies."

"Like coffee mornings," Josser suggested.

"No! Nothing like them," Ferriter said, "But I do know dogs have a fondness for biting when they're let off their leads."

"I'm not going," Mel said.

"Oh, you don't have to worry. I'll be bringing along some pepper."

"Why not salt?" Mel asked. "Give the dog a real treat?"

Ferriter turned to Josser and said, "Sometimes he's exactly like you. Most disappointing."

"When do we go?" Josser asked.

Cherry, feeling very self-important, led them to Poges Minor, and once they were past the 'Bap and Bottle', Ferriter took charge. Fortunately, all the dogs they saw were on leads, tied to gateposts or bicycles, or half asleep. When they came to the huge gates of the big house they had to wriggle through the bars. Ferriter told then to wait in the shadow of the nearby trees until dark. If they tried crossing the lawns in broad daylight the 'vultures might have a go at them'. Mel was even more alarmed.

"They're only crows," Ferriter whispered to Josser, "But I do like frightening Mel."

Cherry stared at the big house. He admitted that he could not remember which room he had been in but it must be on the second floor because he looked down at the lawns.

"And what else," Ferriter asked.

"Trees."

"You have a lot to learn," Ferriter told him.

"Something that stood out because it was only one," Mel suggested.

"And don't say the sun," Josser advised.

"Well, there was a gardener," Cherry ventured and there was very long silence before Ferriter said, "Maybe we should bang on the front door and ask."

"I would like to see the front door," Josser said wistfully.

"The gardener was pulling weeds out of a fountain," Cherry told them.

"I hope you don't talk like that on purpose," Ferriter said.

"And red ivy," Cherry added. "All round the window."

"Now we can go scouting," Ferriter declared.

Even though the light had almost faded into darkness before they reached the foot of the wall they could all see a very safe climb through the ivy to reach the window.

"You'll see books on a shelf," Cherry whispered.

"Now you're learning," Ferriter said.

"And I want to do this," Cherry insisted.

"You don't go in," Josser told him firmly. "Just push the letter through the window and come down." He waited with Mel while their two companions scrambled up to the window. Ferriter was the first to come down.

"The right room," he said. "That lad is sharp. Right now he's pushing that letter through a gap between the frame and the window. Then we're off. Where's Josser?"

At that moment they saw the glare of headlights as a car pulled up at the gates. Cherry scrambled down to join them. "Done it!" he said triumphantly. "Where's Josser?" They heard the screech as the gates were opened, and then the noise of a car approaching the house.

"You get out of here," Mel urged. "I know where to find him."

Mel had guessed right. Josser had sneaked away to gaze at the front door. There he was, standing in the drive, lost in admiration, as he stared up at exactly the kind of front door he had desired in his wildest dreams. The car, now moving quite quickly, was heading directly for him. Mel yelled and rushed. He grabbed Josser and, closing his eyes, bundled both of them out of the way. They staggered and tumbled, falling in a heap behind a very large flower pot. The car came to a stop right where Josser had been standing. The doors opened and they heard a voice they knew well.

"Papa, you almost ran over a rabbit."

"Did I, my dear? You mean I missed it? What a pity. Cook could have made fricassee au lapin."

"Papa! That is horrible!"

They heard another door open. Someone groaned and there was a dull thud. They heard another voice.

"Penelope, why is Icarus lying face down on the gravel?"

"He fell out of the car, mama. He is feeling sick."

"Not again. Ambrose, I told you driving non-stop from Carlisle was not a good idea."

There was a loud sigh before the same voice went on, "Penelope, darling, take your brother up to his bedroom and don't let him be sick on the stair carpet. We've just had it cleaned."

"Yes, mama."

"Nice to back home, my dear?" It was the man again.

"Well, my dear, ask me after I've had a reviving G and T."

They heard the sound of more steps and few groans, followed by the man's voice again.

"William, be a good fellow, and carry our bags into the hall. Then you can take the car round the back, go into the kitchen and enjoy a slice of cook's excellent sausage pie." That word 'sausage' made Josser sit up so quickly he banged his head against the flower pot. Mel had to hold him tightly so he didn't fall sideways and be seen. They remained where they were until William had driven the car away and everything was quiet.

"Go home now," Mel whispered. With his stunned brother clinging on to his arm, he began the long trudge back to the Low Wood. When they reached the 'Bap and Bottle' Josser had to stop and lie down under a picnic table. Mel went foraging and returned with a half empty crushed carton of apple juice and a screwed-up bag containing a few cheese and onion crisps. Josser said he felt better and they set off again, but then Josser complained he felt wobbly and fell over again.

When he woke up he was lying on a soft bed of straw and staring up at the branches of his own oak tree.

"Welcome back," Mel said, before telling his brother that Ferriter, having made sure Cherry was home and safe, came back to look for them, accompanied by Clogs. They had cut some sticks from a hedge, improvised a stretcher and carried Josser home. He had slept all the way.

"And snored," Mel said to round of his story.

While Mel went fishing Josser tried to work on his door and became very annoyed with himself when he could not remember what he must do next.

"It's completely gone out of my head," he told Mel.

"Knocked out by a flower pot. You banged your head against a very big one."

"Why would I want to do that?"

"You heard someone say 'sausage'.

Josser remembered.

"Sausage pie! PALS family can afford to eat sausage pie! What is sausage pie?" He frowned. "You knocked me over. I do remember that. It hurt."

"To save you from being smeared by a big car."

"Why should I be smeared?"

"Because you were standing in the way, and staring at a front door."

"Door! It's come back!" Josser was on his feet and trying to put on his hat.

"Where are you going now?" Mel asked.

"To talk to Tecky. Not sure why, but I need to talk to him."

"You're mad," Mel protested. "You still ill. You're unhinged."

"That's it! Unhinged! Hinges!" said Josser. "I remember everything now." And then he was off.

Special occasions, which were not as important as confabs or Kissmas, did not require invitations or programmes. Everyone knew Josser was going to celebrate the opening of his new door. They could attend or stay away as they pleased. Limpet said he was definitely not going, though everybody knew he would certainly be there. There were only two unknowns. Would Josser paint his door yellow or purple? Would the biggie appear? The second question was answered when Pipkin found a very short message taped to the gate. When he turned it the right way up it

126

read 'Yes.' Then Josser himself changed colour, turning a very deep brown and Mel had to explain the door was not being painted but stained with walnut juice. Boff was shocked.

"A walnut door under an oak tree! Ridiculous," he shouted. "Where has he put the letter box? Right at the top?"

"Don't tell anyone I've told you," Mel whispered, "But it's at the very bottom, like at the big house."

Tecky came to do one final job, which was to hang the door on its hinges. He went away shaking his head. "I don't think I want to watch," he said. Mel was given a preview because he had a minor role to play.

"I walk inside and close the door," Josser explained. "You wait a little while and then bang on the door knocker. Simple."

Mel looked at the door. It seemed to be tilting.

"Shouldn't it be upright?" he asked.

"Only when it's closed," Josser said.

"I've brought my cushion," Penny said when she met Mel at the gate, and showed him a bright yellow cushion with tassels.

"I have to blindfold you," Mel warned.

"That's silly," Penny said, but she obeyed, and was guided to the oak tree where a small crowd was already waiting. Lib and Lus insisted on sharing her cushion because they were her very best friends.

"It's like a play," Penny whispered.

"I hope not," Mel said, remembering the last one. Yappo called for silence and then Josser explained what he was about to do before unveiling his door. There was a gasp when the bedsheet was pulled aside. Someone clapped. Others joined in as Josser walked proudly into his house. He tried to close the door but it would not budge until Mel and Boff helped by pushing. After much screeching it closed, but it also sagged and cracked.

"It's come off a hinge," Boff whispered. Mel counted to twenty, as agreed, and banged hard on the knocker. It fell off.

They heard muffled noises from inside.

"I think he wants us to pull," Boff said. He grabbed hold of the doorknob and pulled. It came away in his hand and he fell over. The crowd cheered.

"Reckon he's stuck," Streaky shouted.

"He'll never get out and I won't get my nails back," Limpet yelled because he was also there, having promised he would not attend.

"He'll starve to death, the poor thing," Mrs. Mangle said, not sounding at all sad.

"Feed him a bacon sandwich through the letter box," Clogs suggested.

"Take the bacon out first," Streaky said. The noise from inside became very loud; it sounded as if Josser was trying to kick his way through his door. The crowd laughed. They cheered when Boff sent Pipkin to fetch his biggest sledgehammer. Mrs Gaffer, who was pretending not to be amused, observed that Josser had even managed to exceed his Kissmas performance. Then they all sat back to watch Boff demolish the door with his sledgehammer so Josser could step out, remove his hat and bow. Auntie Bessiburger led the applause by shouting, "Brill! Encore!"

"Is it always like that?" Penny asked when Mel had taken her back to the gate and she could remove her blindfold.

Mel smiled and said, "Only when Josser is awake."

Penny scrambled over the gate and turned.

"You have given me a lot of questions. How about answering one of mine? When I asked Cherry if he was a dwarf, he was puzzled and answered he was just Cherry. What else could he be?"

"You call us dwarfs," Mel said. "You call us gnomes, goblins, hobgoblins, pixies, leprechauns. Any names you can think up, and you even invent us like Bilbo Baggins, Ariel, the Seven Dwarfs or that weird creation in Peter Pan."

"Oh. Yes. I remember. Tinkerbell," Penny giggled. "Josser would make a real mess of that word"

"All fiction." Mel told her, "And you do the same to real people. You call yourselves white, black, brown, red, or yellow. But you do that to be different. We want to be us. The same. People. Just people."

"So you can enjoy being different," Penny said. "I think I understand."